GRUMP IN A KILT

A GRUMPY SOFT FOR SUNSHINE SMALL TOWN SCOTTISH ROMANCE

KILTED HEARTS

BOOK TWO

KAIT NOLAN

TAKE THE LEAP PUBLISHING

ONE

On a good day, Malcolm Niall hated parties.

And people.

And peopling.

Today was about as far from a good day as it was possible to get.

How could anybody expect him to celebrate anything on The Anniversary? Not that anyone here was aware of the significance of the date. The one person who knew had willfully disappeared without a trace. Malcolm didn't allow himself to think about young Afton Lennox. She was just another person he'd failed. The former Baroness of Lochmara had escaped from the prospect of an arranged marriage by gambling away her entire estate and title to an American. Raleigh Beaumont.

No one had expected Raleigh to stick once he found out about the centuries-old marriage pact that meant he had to marry Kyla MacKean, heiress to the neighboring estate of Ardinmuir, or lose Lochmara entirely. Instead, the two had eloped and, shockingly, actually fallen for each other. Malcolm had known Kyla since she was a wee girl, as he did her brother, Connor, who'd been meant to wed Afton. Kyla and Raleigh did actually seem to suit each other, which was one of the few silver linings to the chaos of the past months.

She was currently distracting her husband from the surprise birthday party being set up here on the grounds.

Malcolm had wanted to dislike the Yank on principle, but he was forced to admit—at least to himself—that his new boss was not at all what he'd expected. The man was a hard worker and had a heart the size of his native Texas, maybe because he'd grown up as part of a ranching family. He could've come in and made a boatload of changes to the estate and how it ran. Instead, he'd taken a learner's mindset, seeing how things were done here in Scotland and respecting Malcolm's near twenty years of expertise as the estate manager. On top of that, Raleigh had invested in the ventures of a number of his tenants, allowing them to expand their various businesses.

But his few months of observation were apparently over, and he was beginning to make changes with an eye toward longevity and environmental sustainability for the future of the estate. Malcolm was a man of nature, so he could appreciate Raleigh's motivation, but why the bloody hell did everything have to change right now? Hadn't there been enough upheaval?

"Put that table over there, will you darlin'? We're gonna bring out the appetizers here in a little bit."

The sound of that easy Southern drawl had Malcolm's shoulders twitching tight with irritation, even as his gaze was pulled toward the tiny Latina spitfire who'd made his life one step away from a living hell.

Charlotte Vasquez, Raleigh's self-proclaimed second mother, had followed him to Scotland. The woman drove Malcolm absolutely crazy. She was smiley and cheerful and pushy—his absolute antithesis. That was all bad enough, but damn if she didn't have a sharp tongue and utter refusal to take shit off anyone—including him—that Malcolm couldn't help but find sexy as hell. The physical package didn't hurt there, either. She was a wee thing, not even topping his shoulders, but despite her diminutive stature, she had generous curves in all the right places. She was the kind of woman a man wanted to get his hands on. Then there were those dark eyes that invited you to drown in them, and all that thick, black hair his fingers itched to touch.

Not that he'd do any such thing, because he didn't actually like the woman. And she was his boss's mother. Sort of.

Maybe he could've gotten past that for some sort of short-term tumble, but Charlotte wasn't going home to Texas. She was staying in Scotland, with plans to ruin his sanctuary by turning the big manor house of Lochmara into a bed-and-breakfast. If she got her way, strangers would be running around all the time.

He didn't want strangers around.

They'd talk to him and expect an answer.

"Can I get a hand over here?"

Case in point.

But Malcolm trudged over to the truck that had been used to haul tables and chairs from the event planning business Kyla and her friend Sophie ran at Ardinmuir. Raleigh's friend Zeke, who'd flown over from America for this party, had one of the long tables dragged almost all the way out. Malcolm picked up the other end and helped him cart it into the formal gardens where the party was being held.

At least the B&B was on down the line.

Right now, the focus was on rehabbing and renovating the empty crofters' cottages at Lochmara and Ardinmuir into spaces that could be rented out to tourists. That prospect didn't bother Malcolm quite as much. He recognized the need for diversification in order to sustain the estates, and the cottages weren't nearby enough to put strangers on his doorstep.

In the beginning, the focus had been on the twenty or so cottages at Ardinmuir, so Charlotte had spent her time driving Connor crazy with her "vision" for the whole thing. But over the past month, Connor and his small crew more or less had a handle on things at his estate, so the project had bled over to Lochmara.

Which meant Malcolm was now working with Charlotte more or less daily, and he was essentially at the end of his rope.

They didn't agree on anything. He was practical. She was fanciful, more concerned with form over function. Malcolm was exhausted from all the head-butting. And as if that wasn't bad enough, she'd moved into the other half of the duplex where he lived on the estate, which meant he couldn't escape her anywhere.

The last thing he wanted was to spend any time at this stupid party. He'd finish helping with setup, wait until the surprise was sprung, wish Raleigh a happy birthday, and then get the hell out.

He moved and carried whatever needed moving and carrying, from outdoor furniture to coolers, to food being set upon the now cloth-covered tables. Then, at last, everything was set, and the crowd of guests took their positions, ducking behind shrubs and tables.

Malcolm found himself next to Ewan McBride, one of the MacKeans' cousins, who owned The Stag's Head Pub in the nearby village of Glenlaig. As the minutes drew out, the younger man pulled a flask from his pocket and offered it.

Malcolm shook his head. He'd be drinking tonight, but it wouldn't be here.

He shifted, his aging knees complaining about the sustained crouch. "I dinna ken what's taking so long."

Ewan grinned. "They're newlyweds. What do you think?"

That supposition seemed to be confirmed when the happy couple finally materialized a full twenty minutes after the designated start-time. Both looked fresh from a shower.

"Somebody's already got one of his birthday presents," Ewan muttered in a low voice.

As soon as Raleigh and Kyla entered the garden, they all leapt up, shouting, "Surprise!"

The wave of sound made Malcolm flinch. There were too many people. Too much happy.

Raleigh began making the rounds, shaking hands, thanking people for coming.

Malcolm considered trying to push closer to get this part over with, but if he'd learned nothing else about Raleigh, it was that the man could talk. He probably got that from Charlotte.

"Zeke!" Raleigh's shout of excitement was followed by the two men embracing with back-thumping hugs. "I can't believe you're here!"

"Couldn't miss it."

Somebody turned on the sound system, and music began to pump through the garden. Raleigh continued to make his way through the crowd. And suddenly Malcolm couldn't take it anymore. He needed to get the fuck out of here.

With all the focus on the birthday boy, it was easy to slip away. With everyone else there, it wasn't as if Raleigh was likely to notice or care that Malcolm didn't wish him a proper happy birthday. It wasn't as if they were mates.

His flat was a hundred or so meters from the manor house. Near to the stables, the building had once housed stable staff. Sometime in the past fifty years, it had been converted into two flats. With the noise of the party at his back, Malcolm unlocked his door and stepped inside. The heavy paneled wood muted the sounds of celebration enough that he could breathe a little sigh of relief.

There were no more eyes on him. No more performing. No more pretending that his world wasn't bleak and barren right now. He didn't have to hide the grief that was a constant companion.

Moving with purpose, he strode to the little kitchenette and opened the cabinet above the refrigerator. An old and dusty bottle of Macallan sat on the shelf. He pulled it out, as he had many times over the years. But instead of inspecting it, challenging himself, then putting it away again, this time he grabbed a glass. The pop of the cork as he opened it ignited a whole host of memories he'd done his best to forget. But tonight, those were preferable company.

Tipping the bottle, he poured himself a glass and prepared to get blind, stinking drunk for the first time in twenty years.

———

Charlotte Vasquez loved parties.

And people.

And peopling.

She fed off bringing people joy and making them comfortable. It was what had attracted her to the hospitality industry, once upon a very long time ago. She'd loved a lot of things about her job as a corporate executive for a big hotel chain. It had been a hell of an achievement as the first college graduate in her family. Papi had been so proud.

But none of that had stopped her from walking away when her lifelong best friend had been given a terminal diagnosis. She'd never regretted that decision, never regretted the choice to stay for Raleigh, even though it had cost her that career and the chance for a marriage and children of her own. They made their own family, and unconventional though it was, it worked for them.

Moments like this one, when she watched her boy pull his best friend in for a back-slapping hug as he grinned from ear to ear, made it absolutely worth it. She was glad Zeke had been able to get away for another trip across the pond so soon. He'd flown out back in the spring to be a witness for Raleigh's wedding, and he'd jumped at the chance to come back. By his own admission, that had only been half about Raleigh. Zeke had his sights set on more of the small-batch artisan cheese made by one of Lochmara's crofters, Pippa Wallace. Charlotte privately wondered whether that was more to do with Zeke's heart than his stomach. He was an incorrigible flirt, so she suspected it would take him a while to figure out the difference. She certainly looked forward to the show.

Pulling her attention away from the embracing men, Charlotte scanned the assembly, automatically assessing whether any of the guests needed anything. Someone had started the music, and hands were already full of drinks. That had been the easiest way to quell the restless crowd when Kyla took longer than planned to get Raleigh down for the party. Everyone seemed content and happy to be here, except for one lone figure, trudging away into the dark, kilt swishing as he walked.

Though she couldn't see his face, she'd recognize that hulking form anywhere. Tall, with broad shoulders, Malcolm was a mountain of a man. She'd had more than one fantasy about him wielding a broadsword since she'd met him. He was exactly what she pictured for the brawny Scottish warrior heroes in the historical romances she enjoyed. It was too damned bad that his attitude was permanently dialed to Grumpasaurus Rex. He had a chip on his shoulder the size of Scotland, and Charlotte really wished that did more to detract from his overall sex appeal than it did. He didn't like her, didn't appreciate her input on the renovations they were both working on. The man had to fight her every step of the way. If he were left in charge, the cottages would end up resembling monastic cells rather than cozy homes away from home that invited guests to stay awhile. Which was the entire point of the endeavor. Their uneasy partnership was saved from utter disaster by the fact that he was capable and competent, traits she appreciated in those she worked with, despite whatever attitude they came with.

As she watched him walk away, her knee-jerk irritation faded. There was something in his posture, in the way those massive shoulders bowed, that told her this was more than his usual aversion to social gatherings. She couldn't quite put her finger on why, but she sensed he was struggling somehow. Pain recognized pain.

For just a moment, she considered going to check on him.

But he wouldn't welcome the intrusion, and the party was in full swing. It was her boy's birthday, and she wanted to celebrate.

She wandered over to the cake table, where Angus MacKean, Kyla's great uncle, was holding court beside the confection of butter, sugar, and flour he'd made for the occasion. His cheeks were flushed with pleasure and lively amusement. It was a far cry from how he'd looked after his heart attack a few months before.

"Angus, as good as this cake looks, I expect you're having to beat people off with a stick."

He grinned. "Could be we should ask Raleigh whether he wants to start with dessert first."

Charlotte looped her arm through his. "It's a wise man who does. Especially during a celebration."

They both looked over to where Raleigh was still greeting guests, one hand tight around his wife's.

"There is definitely a lot to celebrate," Angus agreed.

"I'll drink to that." She lifted her glass of sparkling cider and tapped it to his.

There were so many things to be thankful for, which was an enormous surprise, considering where they'd both been six months ago. Everyone had been shocked when Raleigh's father died and left everything, including the family ranch that was his son's legacy through Lily, to his second wife. Charlotte had always thought Luther Beaumont was a bastard, but even she hadn't been prepared for that. They'd both been out on their asses within a week.

Now, here they were, in a whole other country, building new lives. Raleigh was not only married, he was happy. She could see it in every line of his posture, every nuance of his face. No mother could ask for more for her son.

They both went back to watching Raleigh and Kyla work the crowd.

"He's been so good for her," Angus observed.

"And she for him. Who would've thought that would be the result of an arranged marriage?"

"It's certainly no' how Connor and Afton would have turned out, had they gone through with it."

She turned her attention back to Angus. "How is Connor about all of this? It's got to be an enormous change for him, being free to pursue someone for love."

"I'm not sure if he's quite ready for that."

"Not ready to give up his playboy ways?" She'd heard some stories of Connor's exploits.

"Actually, I'm no' sure he's sought any female companionship since before the wedding. If he has, he's keeping mum about it. I think he's still wrapping his head around the idea that he could have a real relationship with someone."

Turning her attention back to the party, Charlotte searched Connor out, finally locating him in conversation with Hamish Colquhoun, the lawyer who'd handled all the details of the estate transition. His focus was on someone else. Following Connor's gaze, she spotted Sophie Cameron, Kyla's best friend and business partner, laughing with Pippa Wallace. Charlotte's inner romantic sat up and said, *hmmm.*

"Charlotte!" Across the garden, Raleigh lifted his hand in a come-hither gesture. "There's somebody I want you to meet."

She bussed Angus's wrinkled cheek. "Duty calls. I'll see if I can nudge him in this direction so we can all get into that beautiful cake of yours."

The evening rolled on in a blur of faces and names. Food was eaten, beverages were consumed, and the center of the garden was turned into a makeshift dance floor. By the end of the night, Charlotte decided her first official party in Scotland was a massive success. As the guests began to make their way toward vehicles, the hostess energy that had fueled all the prep and setup and socializing began to wane. The idea of all the teardown left her feeling exhausted.

Kyla slipped an arm around her waist. "Why don't you let all of us do the cleanup? You put in the most work of anybody to plan this."

Under ordinary circumstances, Charlotte would have ignored the offer and seen everything cleaned up, but she was tired from more than simply party planning. She was happy to be here and thrilled beyond belief that Raleigh was settled and happy himself. But there was grief, too, that Lily hadn't lived to see this.

"I won't say no. I'm sure I'll see y'all tomorrow."

"Night, Charlotte."

She found Raleigh. "I'm giving you one more birthday hug and then turning in."

He wrapped her in a tight embrace. "It was an awesome party. I'll even forgive you for making it a surprise party, when you know I hate surprises."

"If you're telling me Kyla didn't spill the beans, then I'll have to up my estimation of her secret-keeping abilities."

The look on his face had her laughing. She rose to her toes and pressed a noisy kiss to his cheek. "Good night, sweet boy. Happy birthday."

"Love you."

"Love you back."

Abandoning the younger folks to cleanup, she headed to her flat.

The tequila she'd bought earlier in the week, in anticipation of exactly this night, was waiting on the counter of the kitchenette. It was her tradition to have a drink with Lily every year on Raleigh's birthday and after all his milestones. She'd been doing it for years, sharing those moments with her friend in the only way she knew how.

Crossing to the cabinet, she pulled out a glass and picked up the bottle. She'd already had alcohol tonight, so this would be just one shot in honor of Lily.

Something thumped through the wall.

Malcolm was still up.

Charlotte thought of the bowing in his shoulders and felt a fresh surge of concern. He wouldn't appreciate what he'd deem her nosiness, but she found she couldn't just shrug it off. She'd go check on him, even though it would likely result in him slamming the door in her face.

Without giving herself a chance to think, she snagged another glass and took the lot of it next door.

Two

After a fifth of whisky, Malcolm's blood was swimming. Or maybe that was his head. He wasn't entirely sure, but he definitely recognized the clear attraction he felt to this numbing sensation. The pain that was his constant companion had gone quiet. Even through the haze of alcohol, he understood that this was how he'd fallen into the bottle all those years ago. Trying to escape down the rabbit hole. Through the looking glass. Or something.

He eyed his empty glass and picked up the bottle to pour another. When only a single drop rolled out, he closed one eye and squinted into the narrow neck, as if that would explain what had happened to the whisky. Neither the glass nor the bottle was refilling itself. Before he could decide what to do about that, someone knocked on the door.

Malcolm recognized he wasn't in fit condition to handle anything, but as he was the estate manager, whatever it was fell to him anyway, so he pushed himself to unsteady feet and stumbled to the door. He really hoped nobody had gone off into a ditch and needed their vehicle pulled out with one of the 4x4s or the tractor.

Charlotte stood on the stoop, the faint glow of the exterior light by her own door casting a small halo over her dark hair. She looked like some kind of angel, which put Malcolm's back up.

"Why are you here?"

As usual, she didn't even flinch at his impersonation of a bear. "I noticed you left the party early, so I came to check on you."

He scowled. He didn't need anything from this woman who made him want things he couldn't have. "Why would you do that?"

On a shrug, she lifted something. "I thought you might like to have a drink with me."

His gaze tracked the squat bottle in her hand. The liquid inside was paler than the whisky he'd been drinking, but beggars couldn't be choosers. If the gods wanted to gift him this ready supply, he shouldn't turn it away.

A very quiet voice in the back of his mind shouted that this was a terrible idea because he had no business drinking any more, regardless. Plus, he didn't actually *like* this woman.

But she was so bonnie, and she smelled nice, and that southern drawl did things to him, so he found himself stepping back to allow her inside.

She walked over to the coffee table, where he'd left his glass and empty whisky bottle. Without comment, she dropped onto the sofa—the only place to sit in the tiny lounge—and poured them each a glass. Look at her, being all prepared. She'd brought one for each of them!

Setting the bottle down with a thump, she held one of the glasses out to him.

Concentrating very hard on walking, because the floor seemed to pitch a little with every step, he crossed to her and took it.

Charlotte lifted her own. "*Salud.*"

"*Slainte.*"

They both tossed back the contents.

Malcolm wheezed a cough as the liquid fire hit his chest. "What the bloody hell is this?"

"Tequila."

Definitely not his normal drink. Not that he had a normal drink anymore. He seldom had more than a pint at the pub, and that no more than once a month. But tonight was about breaking all his rules, so he'd embrace the chaos.

With that in mind, he let himself look at her, drinking in all that thick hair, those lush curves. And even through the film of alcohol, he registered the sadness. Without his defenses in the way, he recognized that this was not the normal, bubbly Charlotte he was accustomed to. Right in this moment, there was no bright, happy mask in place, just the pain underneath. He saw it in her as clearly as he felt it in himself, and he found he hated the idea of something hurting her. He wanted to know what had happened, so he could go beat someone's ass to make it right.

Carefully, he lowered himself to the other end of the sofa. "Why are you drinking tonight?"

She poured herself another shot. "Tradition, partly. Raleigh's birthday is a tough day for me. Well, all of his milestones have been hard, because his mom isn't here to see them and share the joy."

Confused, Malcolm held out his glass for a refill. "What does that have to do with you?"

"Lily and I were best friends from the time we were little girls. We figured we'd end up marrying at the same time, buying houses next to each other, having kids together, and growing old together as one big extended family. But that wasn't how it happened. She married Raleigh's daddy, who absolutely didn't deserve her, straight out of high school. Had Raleigh right off. And things were fine for a while. I ended up doing the career thing instead of the marriage and family track. Then she got sick." When her voice hitched, Charlotte drank again, slower this time.

Malcolm's gut clenched because he instinctively understood where this was going.

"It was bad. Cancer. Luther couldn't handle it and checked out, so I took a leave of absence and moved in to take care of her. I was the one who took her to all the doctor's appointments, helping to oversee and manage her treatment and take care of her son through all the grueling, horrific months. Until she ran out of fight." She swallowed the rest of the glass, and when she'd finished, grief had carved lines around her mouth and eyes. "There's not much worse than losing someone you love by degrees."

God, he felt that on a visceral level. He knew it. He'd lived it first hand. And it had all but killed him. For a long time after, he'd wished it had. Some days, he still did.

He never would have imagined that they'd both be members of this terrible club of knowing.

Charlotte twitched her shoulders and set the glass down, linking her hands. "Anyway, every year on Raleigh's birthday, and whenever he has big life stuff happen—like his wedding—I have a drink with Lily and tell her about how our boy is doing."

She drank as a tribute. A way to remember instead of a way to forget.

How different they were.

"Why did you decide to share that with me?"

The gaze she lifted to his was just a little haunted. For a long time, she said nothing. Then she jerked another shrug. "I don't know. Tonight, it just seemed like you'd get it." She held up the bottle, offering him another shot.

He accepted. "Aye. Aye, I get it."

She refilled her own glass. "So, why are you drinking tonight?"

Malcolm had no intention of telling her. His was a private pain he didn't share with anyone.

But against his will, his mouth opened, and the words spilled out.

"I had a daughter."

———

"I had a daughter."

The past tense of the statement struck Charlotte like a bullet, because absolutely nothing he could say that would lead to that state could be a good thing. Her heart was already aching for him when he spoke again.

"She died. Cancer."

Oh God. To lose a child at all was horrific. To lose one like *that.* To watch the sickness devour her from the inside, robbing her of the bloom of youth, of health...

Charlotte laid a hand on his thigh, needing to offer some sign of connection, to show him he wasn't alone. "God, I'm so sorry. Cancer is the worst fucking thing in the world."

If he noticed her touch, he didn't show it. "I'll drink to that."

She poured them more shots. "Do you want to talk about her?"

He looked like he wanted to say no, and she didn't blame him. But his mouth had other ideas.

"Her name was Miranda. She was a bonnie little thing. All full of smiles and sunshine. She loved stuffed animals and cartoons. She had a particular fondness for the *Powerpuff Girls.*" His mouth twisted in a parody of a smile. "She wanted to be Blossom because Blossom was fierce. But I always thought she would be more like Bubbles because she was so bright and happy. She was eight when she died."

Every word was just another gut shot. Obviously, this was the reason for his perpetually surly attitude. Because he'd lost a child. A young one. If ever there was a reason to be the kind of grumpy he was, this was it.

Charlotte didn't think he was aware of the tears streaming down his cheeks. She couldn't stop herself from scooting closer and hugging him, though she had every expectation he'd push her away.

Instead, he wrapped those big, strong arms around her and buried his face in her hair.

She held on tighter. "How long?"

"Twenty years today."

It was the anniversary of his daughter's death. No wonder he hadn't wanted to celebrate. And how incredibly terrible the timing, that this should be Raleigh's birthday. Charlotte did a little hazy math in her inebriated brain and realized that if Miranda had lived, she'd have been almost Raleigh's age.

Her gaze slid to the whisky bottle on the table. She hadn't thought much of it when she'd come in, but with this new information, she realized there was a very good chance it had been full when he started. And she'd given him three shots of tequila on top of that.

Okay, no more alcohol for either of us.

They held each other for a long time, well past the point her back began to ache from the angle. But Charlotte didn't move. If ever someone needed comfort, it was this man, in this moment. And it wasn't exactly a hardship to be pressed close to all that heat and muscle.

At length, he turned his head, nuzzling her neck. "Why do you always smell so good?"

Despite the frisson of heat that shuddered through her at the brush of his skin against hers, alarm bells began to clang in the back of her mind. Of the two of them, she was the more sober. This was absolutely not a good idea.

With one last squeeze, she pulled back. "I think you need to go to bed. It's been a long day. A rough day."

"Okay."

It became rapidly apparent he was not going to get to the bedroom under his own steam. Charlotte eyed the narrow stairway and wondered if she could possibly get him up it or if she ought to leave him down here. Presuming this flat was laid out as hers, the only bathroom was upstairs. He'd need that later. Better he be closer to it.

"On your feet, Malcolm."

"Bossy." He staggered up from the sofa. "Why do I like that?"

"Because it's a wise man who appreciates a woman who knows what she wants." She wedged her shoulder under his armpit and wrapped an arm around his waist. "C'mon."

As she struggled to get him up the stairs, she reflected that the massive size she so appreciated looking at was a whole other thing when said size was one step above deadweight and not in full control of itself. There were a few terrifying moments she thought he might tumble backward down the stairs and break his neck, likely taking her with him, but at last she got him into the bedroom.

She tried to steer him toward the bed—neatly made, she was surprised to see—but he plopped down into a nearby chair instead.

Okay, fine, she could work with this. Carefully kneeling—because she felt that third shot herself now—Charlotte unlaced his boots and tugged them off. Good lord, the man had enormous feet. Everything about him was huge compared to her. Sitting down, he was almost as tall as she was standing. She wondered if other parts of him lived up to the promise. Even in her inebriated state, she knew looking under his kilt to check would cross a line, so she tugged his T-shirt up and off.

He had tattoos high on one shoulder and along the curve of his other biceps. Her fingers itched to trace the designs and the muscles they highlighted, but that, too, would cross a line. Moving away from temptation, she crossed to the bed and pulled back the covers. Now she just had to pour him in. He could sleep in his kilt.

"Okay, just a few more feet."

She got him up again and navigated him toward the waiting bed.

His arm was heavy where it curved around her shoulders. "I'm glad you came over."

"I think I am, too." Their legs bumped the edge of the bed. "Here we go."

"Oh, good. I dinna want to be alone."

Then he toppled like a tree, taking her with him.

Charlotte landed on the bed with an *oof*. Malcolm wasn't

quite squishing her, but his bulk was sprawled half on top of her, and one brawny arm curled tight around her waist.

"Um, Malcolm?"

Her only answer was a soft snore in her ear.

She wriggled, trying to ease free of his grip. His only response was to tighten his hold, tucking her against his side like a giant teddy bear.

Well, it wasn't like he'd hang on to her all night. She'd sneak out later when he rolled over. In the meantime, it was rather nice to be held.

Resigning herself to hanging out for a while longer, she toed off her shoes and settled against his pillow.

THREE

The sound of running water pulled Charlotte from a deep, dreamless sleep. She stretched and realized immediately she wasn't in her own bed. These weren't her bamboo sheets, and she was still fully dressed. Then she remembered being tumbled into Malcolm's bed.

Definitely not how her prior fantasies of that had played out. Those had involved fewer clothes and a lot more skin.

So much for waking up and sneaking out before morning.

At least she lived right next door. No walk of shame necessary. The likelihood that anyone had seen her come over here last night was low, and the doors to the duplex couldn't be seen from the manor house.

She'd slept surprisingly well, all snugged up in his bed. It had been a long damned time since she'd shared sleep—or anything else—with anyone, and apparently some part of her had appreciated the closeness. She could admit to herself she really missed being held. And being held by a man as big as Malcolm was an extra pleasure. Whether he'd intended it or not, having him wrapped around her had made her feel safe. She hadn't realized how much she needed that.

Her brain felt fuzzy, and her head ached. That was what she

got for three shots of tequila on top of the cider she'd had at the party. But, all in all, she didn't feel too terrible.

Evidently, her bedmate was up and banging around the bathroom. How awkward was this conversation about to be? He'd been vulnerable with her last night, something she knew he'd *never* have done sober. Would it change anything between them? Or would he go back to the way things were before?

Did she want it to change something? A part of her wouldn't have minded sharing his bed on a more regular—and active—basis, but that was a lot more complicated since she lived here now. Starting something up with him would probably be a supremely bad idea. If it imploded, as it undoubtedly would, things might get weird for Malcolm with Raleigh. Charlotte didn't want that.

What time was it, anyway? It was hard to tell from the pale slant of sunlight through the bedroom window. The days here were so much shorter than Texas this time of year.

From her cozy spot beneath the covers, she scanned what she could see of his room. It was as spartan up here as it was below. A bed, a nightstand, a tall chest of drawers she'd learned was called a Scotch dresser. There was no artwork. No photographs. Nothing of softness or the personal. She saw a few books stacked on top of the dresser and piled on the nightstand, but she couldn't read the titles from here.

Behind her, the bathroom door opened, and she rolled over. Malcolm stopped dead in the doorway, still wearing nothing but his kilt. Even the ferocious bedhead did nothing to detract from the picture he made. She hadn't fully taken the time to appreciate this view last night, but she took a moment to soak it in now. Long torso, powerful shoulders, strong legs. Age had done nothing but hone his physique, a fact she had to admire, given how many guys she knew his age who'd given in to the dad bod. He really was a ruggedly beautiful man. His usually neatly trimmed goatee was accented by heavy stubble she itched to stroke her fingers over.

Pleased by the idea, she smiled. "Morning."

His poleaxed expression shifted to a fiercer version of his usual scowl. "What the bloody hell are you doing here?"

So, he wasn't pleased to have her in his bed. That shouldn't be demoralizing, under the circumstances. Besides, the man looked really, *really* hung over.

"Well, I helped you to bed last night."

"And thought you'd just help yourself *into* my bed?"

It was her turn to scowl. She'd been here for him last night, damn it. She didn't deserve that accusatory tone. "No. You dragged me down when you fell onto the bed and decided you wanted a teddy bear. You wouldn't let me go, so I decided it would be easier to just go to sleep than to try to fight you. Because in case you've missed the memo, you're twice my size."

He tunneled both hands through his silver-shot brown hair, his face twitching as he processed all of that. Disbelief. Denial. Irritation. "What the hell were you even doing here?"

Either he didn't remember anything about last night—entirely possible since he put away a fifth of whiskey and about half a bottle of tequila—or he was embarrassed about the vulnerability she'd seen and was being a typical male and pushing her away. Either way, she wasn't feeling particularly forgiving at the moment, considering he was looking at her like something to be scraped off his boot.

Her own temper stirring, she shoved upright. "I came to check on you. You seemed like you weren't in a great place. Clearly, you weren't. Neither was I. We had a few drinks. I put you to bed." She threw the covers back and got up, gesturing to the fact that she was still fully clothed, except for the shoes she'd managed to kick off. "Nothing happened."

"Thank fuck. You're the last woman I need to get tangled up with."

His vehemence was a blow to her pride.

She wasn't any more vain than the average woman, and she

certainly didn't need everyone to like her. But she wasn't accustomed to having kindness met with hostility.

"Excuse me?"

"A needy, opportunistic, mother-hen type. Just because the boy you raised is all grown up and disnae need you anymore, dinna think you should start in on everyone else."

The barb landed true, and Charlotte flinched back as if he'd struck her. The ugliness of it hurt so much in the moment, she couldn't even spar back with her usually ready temper.

She wouldn't give him the satisfaction of storming out. Wouldn't let fall the tears stinging the backs of her eyes. With slow deliberation, she bent to pick up her shoes. Straightening her shoulders, she met his angry gaze.

"I apologize for being someone who treated you like you mattered."

With those soft words of reproach ringing between them, she walked out.

———

She was supposed to spar with him. To fight back. Call him the asshole he surely was. That would have put them back into a familiar dynamic and made Malcolm feel like he was more in control.

He desperately needed to feel some control.

Instead, she'd lost several shades of color from the usual warmth of her skin before pulling in on herself, so that she actually looked her diminutive stature instead of the larger-than-life personality that usually filled a room. Her parting words had been soft, and all the more powerful for it.

I apologize for being someone who treated you like you mattered.

When was the last time anyone had done that beyond basic human decency? Not since Afton left.

Malcolm wasn't a people pleaser, and he sure as hell didn't

need anyone to like him. But he wasn't in the business of deliberately inflicting pain. And even through the pounding pulse of agony in his skull and the profound regret about his life choices, he recognized he'd hurt Charlotte. Deeply.

He waited for the inevitable door slam. He'd certainly earned it. But he heard only the telltale squeak of hinges before a quiet click of the latch.

Fuck.

He'd done that.

Diminished her.

Malcolm didn't want to be that guy. That guy was a shithead who was so massively hung over, he lashed out at someone else over his own shame, simply because she was a ready target.

How could he have allowed himself to fall back into the bottle, even for one night? He knew better than to take that risk. To make that choice. And yet, here he was.

He scrubbed both hands over his face, as if that would somehow erase the haze covering his memories of last night.

Why had Charlotte come at all? Why had she stayed? Had he really not let her leave? Heat crawled up the back of his neck at the idea of what she might've read into that.

He'd been in such a dark headspace last night. God knew what he might have told her. What he might have exposed. The vulnerability of that made him extremely uncomfortable. But that was no excuse for what he'd said.

There was no excuse for what he'd said.

He owed Charlotte an apology.

Shite. He hated apologizing—almost as much as he hated people. But he turned toward the stairs to do the thing before he lost his nerve.

The ringing of the phone had a fresh spike of pain lancing through his skull. Swearing a blue streak, he stumbled to answer.

"What?"

A weighted silence followed his snarled greeting.

"Well, good morning to you, too." Raleigh's voice was dry.

"You're usually already up by now. Sorry I woke you. Are we still on for the stock auction today?"

Oh, bloody hell. He was meant to be in a truck with Raleigh all fucking day. Just what would he say if he knew Malcolm had insulted his second mother?

Malcolm could blow the auction off. He felt like warmed over death. As a rancher, Raleigh was more than qualified to pick out new stock. But this was his job, and he never shirked his duties.

"Aye. Half an hour." He hung up and headed downstairs to do what he could to make himself more human. Charlotte's apology would have to wait. It wasn't like he'd be able to find the right words in his current state, anyway.

The sight of the empty whisky bottle on the coffee table filled him with self-revulsion. A part of him wanted to go out and buy more. To fall back into old, destructive patterns. To hide from himself, from the world, behind the shield of chemical numbing.

Instead, he chucked the bottle into the bin and started the coffee and some bacon. As the scent of frying meat filled the room, he downed some painkillers and another tall glass of water. The first cup of coffee he drank black, while frying up some eggs alongside the bacon. By the time he'd shoveled the lot of it in with a second cup of coffee, the headache had bumped down a few notches, such that light and sound no longer made him want to vomit. Progress.

Because he smelled like a distillery, he lurched back upstairs to shower. As the spray beat down on his bowed head, fragments of the night before began to flicker back into his consciousness. Tequila shots. A sense of kinship. Charlotte looking... sad? No, not just sad. She'd lost someone the way he'd lost Miranda, and she'd... comforted him.

Fuck. That made what he'd said all the worse.

No part of him wanted to go anywhere near this. But he knew he couldn't live with himself if he didn't make amends. Somehow.

He was still racking his aching brain for answers when the brisk knock sounded. As he tugged open the door, a heavy sense of dread settled in his stomach as he thought about being trapped with the younger man for the next several hours. What if he wanted to talk? Worse, what if he thought this excursion was some kind of bonding exercise? Or even worse, what if he'd seen Charlotte come over here last night?

Raleigh stood on the stoop in his habitual cowboy getup of jeans, boots, flannel shirt, and hat. At the sight of Malcolm, he rocked back on his heels, one brow arching up. Wisely, he didn't comment on Malcolm's current state.

"You ready to go?"

Malcolm grunted an affirmative. "Just a second."

Needing more fortification for whatever was to come, he poured the last of the coffee into a travel mug and snagged his jacket before stepping out into the chill morning. Looked like they were in for one of those rare, cloudless sunny days. Ugh. He hid his aching eyes behind sunglasses and began striding toward the truck, feeling the ground wobble a little beneath him.

Realizing he still wasn't a hundred percent sober, Malcolm announced, "You're driving."

Raleigh just nodded and heading for the driver's side door. "Okay. Let's get rolling."

FOUR

ow dare *he? I am not needy.*

Charlotte slammed her sledgehammer into the wall and watched in satisfaction as chunks of plaster and pieces of lath rained down. It had taken her a couple of hours to work her way through the hurt, but on the other side of coffee and huevos rancheros, she'd found her way to the mad. Mad was a lot more comfortable. The Vasquez clan had quick, passionate tempers that burned hot, then flamed out. Well, except for her abuela, who was famed for her ability to hold a grudge. Charlotte was pretty sure she just might rival Tita Carlotta on that front after this morning's debacle. So she'd taken one of the estate 4x4s and come out to the next cottage slated for renovation to work off this need for violence. And if she was picturing Malcolm Niall's head on the wall that framed in the microscopic bathroom, well, who could blame her?

"Stubborn, narrow-minded, testosterone-poisoned asshat."

Another shower of plaster and lath fell to the floor under the siege of her hammer. At this rate, she'd have the entire wall demolished in twenty minutes. That would speed along the demo portion of this project. She couldn't do a lot more than that in this cottage until the roof got fixed, and that was, sadly, outside her area of expertise. Plus, there was that unfortunate issue with heights. But she could get the rest of the clearing out done.

Because English wasn't doing the trick for really venting her frustration, she switched to Spanish, letting loose a string of creative insults as she cleaned up debris and a collection of energy bar wrappers someone had left at some point. Then she picked up the hammer again and widened the hole in the wall, blow by blow. The musicality of the language was really so much more satisfying for swearing.

"That looks incredibly cathartic."

Charlotte paused mid-swing to find Sophie in the doorway, hands tucked neatly in the pockets of her fleece vest, gaze focused on the widening hole. "It is." She noted a faint tightness around Sophie's mouth. "You want in on some of this action?"

For a moment, she thought the girl would refuse, then Sophie stepped fully into the cottage. "Can I?"

"Sure. You ever swung a sledgehammer before?"

Sophie shook her head.

Charlotte instructed her on how to hold the hammer and where to stand. "We're taking out this whole wall to prepare for ultimately making the bathroom a little bigger. Pipes run up that exterior wall, so you don't need to worry about damaging those." She stepped out of the way. "Go ahead."

Sophie hefted the hammer and took a clumsy swing at the wall that mostly bounced off where it hit one of the studs. Narrowing her clear grey eyes, she readjusted her grip and stance and swung again, this time caving in a chunk above the hole Charlotte had started.

"Get it, girl!" Charlotte wiped her sleeve over her sweaty brow and reached for the big water bottle she'd brought as she watched Sophie fall into a beautifully destructive rhythm. The girl definitely had something to work off. Charlotte wondered what it was.

She didn't know Sophie well beyond the fact that she and Kyla had opened an event planning business at the MacKean estate of Ardinmuir, and Sophie also ran a flower shop in the village. There was a lovely, bright spirit behind that usually quiet facade that was being smothered by something in her life. It wasn't her friends, so Charlotte concluded it was likely family-related. She didn't know what Sophie's situation was, but it seemed she was short on positive female interaction aside from Kyla. Charlotte was happy to step in and do a little mothering.

Even as the thought struck her, Malcolm's words replayed in her brain.

A needy, opportunistic, mother-hen type. Just because the boy you raised is all grown up and disnae need you anymore, dinna think you should start in on everyone else.

Her hand tightened on the water bottle. It wasn't wrong to care about people, damn it. And there was nothing shameful about the fact that she still had a yearning that had never quite gone away, despite her role in Raleigh's life. She had a lot of love to give to someone. Clearly, that would never be Malcolm Niall.

The jerk.

By the time Sophie stopped several minutes later, sweat beaded along her temple, causing that rich, dark hair to curl a little at her hairline. The tightness around her mouth was gone.

Charlotte handed over another bottle of water. "Feel better?"

"Surprisingly so."

"So, is it a man, work, or family that's got you in a lather?"

Sophie sipped and winced. "I appreciate that you think I have time for a man between work and family obligations."

"Honey, you make time for the good ones—man or woman. So, I take it there's no one special right now?" She thought about Connor MacKean and that long look from last night.

"There's been no one special at all. I dinna have the band-width for a relationship. Not between the shop and all the weddings we've been putting on, and my stepmother—" Sophie cut herself off with another long pull on the water.

"Don't feel like you need to keep mum on my account. I

don't know your step-mama, and as a rule, I've not had reason to be over-fond of any stepmothers. Raleigh's was a raging bitch."

Sophie choked on the water.

Charlotte shrugged. "Well, she was. All I'm sayin' is, if you need to vent, I'm an outsider here and a safe space."

The corner of Sophie's mouth quirked. "I'll tell you mine if you'll tell me yours."

The keenest edge of her anger had already been dulled, so Charlotte jerked her shoulders again and hoped her face didn't betray her discomfort. "Nothing much to tell."

One of Sophie's dark brows winged up. "Are you sure? Because I saw you go into Malcolm's place last night."

Just freaking perfect. Now people are going to be thinking things and making assumptions. Who else just happened to be looking in that direction at that moment?

Deciding to take the bull by the horns, she capped her water. "It's not like that. Nothing happened. I just went over, and we had a drink together. Talked a while. Fell asleep. Woke up this morning, and he was an unmitigated ass, as usual, and said some pretty unforgivable things. I'm pissed off about it, so I'm taking my frustrations out on inanimate objects."

Sophie hummed a quiet, nonjudgmental noise that definitely had the flavor of *methinks the lady doth protest too much.* Or maybe Charlotte was just reading things into her non-reaction, because she let it go.

"I live with my stepmother. She has a lot of... challenges."

"Health challenges?"

"She thinks so. Sometimes it's hard to tell where the line is between legitimate conditions and things she's inflated in her own mind."

"Can't your dad help with that?"

A flash of pain twisted Sophie's features for a moment. "He died several years ago. Heart attack."

Charlotte silently cursed herself for stepping on that land

mine. "Oh, honey. I'm so sorry." Riding on instinct, she stepped in to wrap the younger woman in a tight hug.

After only a moment's hesitation, Sophie squeezed her back, relaxing into the embrace. "Thanks. My stepmother and I don't exactly get on. She disnae like that I look like my mother."

"Because she's reminded of who came before her?"

"Because my mother was Indian. My father was white." She gestured to her eyes. "This is just about the only thing I got from him physically."

"So, your stepmother is a prejudiced bitch?"

"She's... set in her ways."

Charlotte squeezed Sophie's arms. "Honey, don't make excuses for people who belittle you because of the color of your skin. We've got enough people doing that to us without helping them along the way."

"You sound like Kyla and Connor."

"Good. Maybe if enough of us say it, you'll listen. Why do you live with her if she's like that?"

"Partly because I made a promise to my father before he died. Partly because I can't afford to move out and pay for the rent on my shop. Yet, anyway. I hope that'll change with the new wedding business."

"If there's anything at all I can do to help, name it. I'm there. No one should have to live like that."

Sophie's smile bloomed full and lit up her lovely face. "Thank you."

"Why did you come out here, anyway? Were you looking for me?"

"Yes, and no. I finished up the landscaping over at number six and was on my way home when I saw your 4x4. I thought I'd stop in to talk to you about the landscaping plan for a couple of the other cottages."

"You're fabulous at anything that's green and growing, so I'm sure the plans are wonderful, just like all the others."

It was Sophie's turn to twitch her shoulders in a shrug.

"They're not my properties, so I'd just as soon have someone else to confer with. And right now, Kyla's pretty consumed with newlywed bliss."

Charlotte laughed. "You're not wrong. They're not my properties, either, but, of course, I'd be happy to discuss. I love all things design." She passed over a second set of gloves. "Here, put these on and tell me about it while we clear this debris."

———

"Baaaaa!"

Three fuzzy little heads butted Malcolm's legs, demanding attention.

From the other side of the stall door, Raleigh grinned. "I think you're gonna have your hands full with those three."

Because he couldn't very well say he hadn't bought them for himself, Malcolm only grunted and knelt to scratch behind wooly ears.

"Well, if you're good managing the triplets here, I'm gonna head on over to Pippa's to let her know I've picked up another couple of cows to add to the herd."

"You go on. They aren't my first lambs."

With a salute, Raleigh donned his hat and strode out of the barn.

"Baaaa."

"Baa. Baaa!"

Malcolm looked down at the trio of Valais black nose lambs currently trying to climb his legs and wondered what the hell he'd been thinking. Seemed he'd been doing a lot of not thinking the past twenty-four hours. He had no idea what had possessed him to think they'd be a good apology gift, except that he knew Charlotte loved animals, and he couldn't imagine this rambunctious group of babies not making her smile. After he'd shoved his foot well and truly down his throat this morning, he *needed* to bring that smile back, however possible. Presenting her with a trio of the world's cutest, most docile breed of sheep had seemed like a great idea when he'd spotted them at the auction. Now that he had them home, he was questioning his sanity. What if she would've preferred a dog? Or a cat? Or no animals at all?

He couldn't quite imagine that, because she had a massive soft spot for Mabel, the Heilan' coo Raleigh and Kyla had rescued over the summer, who behaved far more like a dog than the cow she was. Now that Mabel had gotten too big to bring into the house, all of them were missing her. Not that the sweet girl ever missed more than a day of play with one of the three of them. And, yeah, okay, Malcolm, too, when no one else was around to see. It was hard not to be amused by a cow that played fetch and loved cuddles.

"Alright, you lot. I'm gonna go get your mum." God, he hoped Charlotte would take this gift as it was intended.

Carefully shutting the babies into the stall, he went in search of her.

She wasn't out playing with Mabel, and she didn't answer the door of her flat. Malcolm debated for about five minutes whether that was because she wasn't home or because it was him on her stoop. Finally deciding there were no signs of life, he headed up to the manor house to check. She often took advantage of the bigger kitchen to cook, something they all benefitted from because, damn, the woman had skills.

He spotted her through the kitchen window and dragged himself to the back door, dread pooling in his gut. Once upon a time, he'd have simply walked on in. He'd been doing it for years. But the house was no longer Afton's, so that didn't feel appropriate. In truth, he struggled to feel welcome in the house now, though Raleigh and Kyla had done nothing to indicate that had changed. And hell, now that they were real newlyweds, walking on in seemed like a dangerous thing to risk. Safer to knock.

Bracing himself, he did exactly that, stepping back off the stoop to wait.

A few moments later, the door swung open. Charlotte filled

the space, dark eyes cool, full lips pressed into a firm line. She said nothing at the sight of him, just waited, a kitchen towel in one hand, her fist propped on the curve of her hip. A streak of something that might have been flour dusted one olive cheek, and he was struck by the absurd urge to wipe it away.

Good way to lose a hand.

He swallowed. "I've got something to show you."

"I'm not really inclined to go anywhere with you, Malcolm."

Beyond embarrassed and utterly ashamed of his behavior, he rubbed at the heat that rose to the back of his neck. "Look, I behaved badly this morning. Please, just come see what I have to show you." The scent of something delicious and full of spices wafted out from behind her. "If you're to a point where you can step away from whatever you're cooking."

Those espresso eyes searched his face. "Fine. Let me just turn the heat down." She disappeared for a few seconds, then came back with empty hands.

Neither of them spoke as he led her back to the barn and down to where he'd stashed the lambs. He jerked his head toward the stall. Confusion flickered over her face, but she stepped up, rising to her toes to look over the stall door.

"Baaa!"

Some of the coldness melted out of Charlotte's face. "Oh, they're darlin'."

"They're yours."

She froze, still on her tiptoes. "I'm sorry, what?"

He shifted, wishing this was over already. "You like animals. I thought you'd enjoy them."

"You bought me sheep?"

"Aye." Malcolm realized she was staring at him as if he'd just announced he'd rented a flat on Mars. Christ, he was an eejit. "If you don't want them, that's fine. We can just make them a part of the regular herd. It was a foolish idea. I just I saw them, and they made me think of you, and I wanted to do something to say that I'm sorry." *Shut up, man.*

She studied him. "Most people would just say I'm sorry."

"I'm not great with words."

"I'm getting that sense." There was no malice in her tone, but he realized she was going to make him spell it out. And she deserved that.

The muscles between his shoulders tensed. "I couldnae remember last night when I woke up. I still dinna remember a lot of it, but I know I made accusations that were wrong and unpardonably cruel. I'm a surly bastard, and I know it. But I try not to be deliberately hateful. I'm sorry."

When was the last time he'd strung this many words together at once?

Charlotte said nothing for so long, he was certain she was calculating the best way of throwing his apology back in his face. He wouldn't have blamed her.

Instead, she opened the latch on the stall and slipped inside, dropping to her butt in the hay. The lambs immediately began to vie for space in her lap, butting for attention. And there was that laugh and the smile he'd reluctantly come to look for every day.

"They're Valais black nose sheep. A Swiss breed. Generally sweet-tempered. I'm told they often behave more like dogs than sheep. I thought, with how much you love Mabel, that they'd suit you."

She cuddled the three of them, eyeing him with an expression he couldn't read. "Well, I suppose as apologies go, this one will do. What are their names?"

The massive tension he'd been carrying around all day released. Malcolm did his best not to show it as he braced his arms atop the stall door and watched them. "That's up to you. They're all female."

"How about Blossom, Bubbles, and Buttercup?"

His throat went thick. This woman. After the abominable way he'd treated her, she'd think to name her lambs after his daughter's favorite characters?

When he said nothing, Charlotte's face softened. "If that's too painful, I can go with something else. Charlie's Angels, maybe."

He shook his head. "No. Miranda would've liked that." His voice went to a rasp. "Thank you."

"You realize you're going to have to teach me how to care for them? I've spent a huge chunk of my life on a ranch, but Rosewood ran cattle, not sheep."

"Aye, I can do that."

And as the feeling of truce settled between them, he considered that he didn't hate the idea of spending more time with her.

Maybe the triplets hadn't been such a bad idea after all.

FIVE

"You... made them an Instagram account?"

In the face of Malcolm's disbelief, Charlotte propped one hand on her hip. "Well, of course I did. They're adorable, and the world needs to see that. Here. Look at all the people being made happy by seeing these three going all boing boing." She opened the app on her phone and showed him the dozens-deep thread of comments on the latest video she'd posted of the triplets losing their wooly little minds over a bubble machine, bouncing around as if they had springs for legs.

One corner of his mouth twitched, which was practically a full-on grin in Malcolm-speak. When he caught her looking, the twitch disappeared, and he handed back her phone. But it was too late. Charlotte had seen his amusement and wouldn't forget it.

"We need to get the painting finished so we can get to furnishing the place."

She picked up a brush and cup of paint and moved to cut in around the new bathroom wall that had been built in the couple of weeks since their detente. "It's not that simple. We need a cohesive look."

He poured paint into a tray and began to load a roller. "What's not simple? It needs beds, a sofa, some chairs. The sooner we get this one done, the sooner they can start taking bookings, and we can move on to the next."

Unable to gesticulate as she wanted because of the paintbrush in her hand, Charlotte settled for a massive roll of her eyes. "You know nothing. *Nothing.* This is not like one of those little hiker shelter bothy things that just provides protection from the elements. We are charging a premium for occupancy and therefore need to offer a premium product. In this case, that product is an experience. People are coming here to experience the Highlands. To taste a little piece of history with the bonus elements of modern conveniences. That means more than simply chucking in a random bed, couch, and chairs."

She couldn't decide if the noise he made was intentionally derisive or not, but felt compelled to make him see it.

"Picture it: You're taking a vacation to some part of the world you've never been to. You want to get away from it all. You arrive at the cozy cottage you booked online to find that it's even better than the pictures, with a wood-burning stove in the corner, a plush sofa that's just made for napping, and a beautiful old rug that's clearly full of stories. The kitchen is adorable—small, but well appointed, with the kettle and coffeemaker you expect, along with a basket of warm beverage fixin's. There's a beautiful wrought-iron tree for mugs—"

"A wrought-iron tree? Like a literal tree?"

"Yes. It's fanciful and fun, while still being practical."

"Where are you going to find something like that?"

"I mentioned it at the last big group dinner you missed. Connor said he might have a line on something for me. Anyway, pay attention. Dinnerware is stacked neatly on open shelves that climb the wall above the counter... Actually, that's a good idea. We should build some, both here and in the bathroom." She scribbled a note on the pad she kept in her back pocket. "Oh, and along that strip of wall between the bedrooms."

"Why are people who are just staying for a weekend gonna need that many shelves?"

"First, people might stay for longer than a weekend, and they need somewhere to put their toiletries and such. Second, we can kit out the cottages with games and artwork and decorative pieces that add to the ambiance. We should get some of Kyla's photographs framed and hang them in each of the cottages, too. It adds to the warmth of the place. Makes it feel like a home away from home."

"Ambiance." This time, he did snort. "What qualifies you as the decision maker about this?"

"The fact that I have more personalization in my flat after two months than you do after God knows how many years. And the years I spent working my way up the ranks in a luxury hotel empire in Texas."

He blinked. "You were in the hospitality industry?"

"Yeah, for fifteen years."

"I... had no idea."

"I don't talk about it much. I took a leave of absence when Lily got sick. And then I elected not to go back when my time was up so that I could stick around for Raleigh."

"Do you ever regret not going back?"

Charlotte hesitated, not because she had to think about her answer, but because she could count on one hand the number of actual real conversations she'd had with this man. He wasn't the sort to ask get-to-know-you questions, so why was he asking now?

"Not most of the time. I started when I was eighteen, while I was in college, and just kept on climbing that ladder, making the jump from management to corporate. The higher I got, the more distance there was from the actual people we were serving. If I'd stayed in, I'd have kept rising, and it would have taken me away from the parts I actually liked about the job."

"What were those?"

"I like taking care of people. Feeding them. Making them comfortable. Anticipating their needs. It's incredibly gratifying to provide someone with a thing they didn't even realize they wanted. Seeing that stress everybody carries around all the time just slide off for a little while."

With a grunt, he bent to refill the paint roller, and Charlotte assumed he was all talked out.

Well, it was a good run. The longest sober conversation they'd had since the day he'd gifted her with the triplets.

"I guess that's why you want to open the B & B at Lochmara."

Surprised, she stopped painting to look at him. "Well, it's why Raleigh gave me the option of opening the B&B. That was actually his idea." And it was no secret that Malcolm absolutely despised the concept.

"It was?"

"Yeah. He knows my strengths. Knows what I like to do. And it's not a terrible idea. The house is perfect for that sort of setup. But I don't know that I want to do it."

"Really?"

"Managing a bed-and-breakfast basically means I'd never be off. That's one of the things I've enjoyed about working as I have. I may not have made a lot of money, but I had time for myself, for relationships that mattered to me. I appreciate that Raleigh's looking for some kind of payback for all those years I gave to him, but I don't need that."

"So, what do you want to do?"

"I don't know. Right now, I'm putting all my focus on getting all these cottages finished and ready to see guests. I think, if it's done well and properly, I can make them profitable enough that managing them and handling all the bookings can be my job. Which would still leave me time and energy to explore other things."

He said nothing for a long time, but for once she understood he was thinking over what she'd said. He was a man who took time to consider things, which she appreciated when he wasn't leaping to wrong conclusions. It was nice having him ask about her rather than making assumptions about who she was as a person.

"Well, I guess if it means guests won't be on my doorstep, I can build the bloody shelves."

Considering it a major win, she smiled sweetly at him. "Thank you."

———

Malcolm pulled up to the cottage, a loaded trailer in tow. He'd grabbed whatever he could carry on his own, leaving the bigger pieces, like mattresses and beds and the sofa, until he could pin down Connor or Raleigh to help with the heavy lifting. He and Charlotte had busted their asses to get this place ready. He'd built the shelves she'd requested, and now they were finally to the furnishing portion of the plan. When he'd left an hour ago, Charlotte had been surrounded by boxes of supplies. Judging by the curl of smoke from the chimney, she'd gotten the wood stove lit. Fair enough. Temperatures had dropped as they rolled into November. Even he had deigned to add a fleece jacket to his usual uniform of kilt and a t-shirt.

He expected to find her fiddling with the placement of some kind of pretty dust catcher, or maybe arranging the books he doubted any of the future guests would read. Instead, he walked in to a mountain of empty boxes and no sign of Charlotte. Maybe she was in the bathroom?

"Oh good, you're back. Come, hold the faucet so it doesn't spin on me."

Malcolm followed the sound of her muffled voice to the tiny kitchen, where he found her wedged beneath the sink.

"What are you doing?"

"Changing the faucet out. What does it look like?"

His gaze dropped to check for water and snagged on the midriff bared by her position. That strip of dusky skin between her sweater and the top of her jeans had his mouth going dry.

That same sweater was pulled taut across her full breasts, making it very clear that each was a perfect one of *his* handfuls, and he itched to test the fit.

Get a grip.

As his brain helpfully supplied an image of him doing exactly that, his cock began to stir.

Not what I meant!

Clearing his throat, he rasped, "I was gonna get to that when I got back."

"But I can do it, so now you don't have to. Just hold the faucet."

Mentally reviewing rugby plays to try to get himself back under control, he did as she asked, clamping the new faucet in place while she tightened the hardware from below with quick efficiency.

"There. Test it."

"You sure you want to be under there when I do?"

"Oh, ye of little faith."

Taking her at her word, Malcolm turned on the water, testing the hot and cold sides and finding everything exactly as it should be. He had to appreciate a competent woman. "Seems to be working."

"I told you." Charlotte edged out from beneath the sink, color streaking across her cheeks as she came eye level with the hem of his kilt.

Before she could say another word—or elect to check what was under said kilt—Malcolm offered her a hand up. The hand she slid into his was tiny but strong, much as the woman herself. She rose easily when he tugged, stumbling a little as she gained her feet. He slid a hand under her other elbow to steady her, which brought her close enough to brush what remained of his erection.

He hastily released her and stepped back, lest it take that as encouragement. "Where did you learn to do this kind of stuff?"

"My daddy and uncle were contractors. I picked up a lot growing up. I know my way around an engine, too, courtesy of another uncle. We didn't have a lot of money, so we learned to take care and repair. No matter who needed help with what, there was always an aunt or uncle or cousin who could lend a hand."

He couldn't imagine. "Your family was close?"

She tossed the wrench back into the toolbox. "Still is. What about you?"

Malcolm had no inclination to talk about where he came from, but he'd been asking lots of questions about her. Telling her something about himself was the expected quid pro quo in this kind of exchange. It was why he usually avoided people.

"Grew up in a council flat in Glasgow. Mum left when I was a wee lad. Da was nothing to write home about. I got out as soon as I was old enough."

"That had to be terrifying. Being on your own like that."

"No' as much as staying." He tensed his shoulders, as if that could shake off the memories. "I scraped by. When Miranda came along, we wanted better for her than scraping by, so we got the hell out of the city."

"We?"

"Robyn. My wife. Ex-wife," he corrected. "We split after..." The words clogged up in his throat. He couldn't even get them out sober. "After."

Charlotte's hand settled on his arm, a warm anchor against memories that wanted to drag him away like the darkest of undertows. "You never get over something like that. You just get through it, surviving one day at a time."

Her eyes were full of so much kindness and understanding. How the hell could he have ever believed she was needy and opportunistic? Was his life so devoid of good that he didn't recognize true empathy when it stared him in the face? She stood close enough he could feel the heat of her. It crossed his mind that he could kiss her. Just haul her to her toes and taste those full lips he couldn't get out of his mind. He didn't think she'd push him away.

But then what? She sure as hell deserved better than the likes of him. A surly, broken, recovering alcoholic.

"I need to unload."

Her hand fell away as he moved toward the door, but she trailed right behind. God, he hoped she wouldn't ask more questions. He needed time to rebuild his walls so that he didn't feel tempted to answer them.

Dropping the ramp of the trailer, he moved inside, dragging a rug off the top of the pile and hefting it atop one shoulder. "Mind your head."

As soon as he cleared the trailer, she went in herself, picking up a side table.

"I'll get it," he insisted.

"I'm not a weakling, Malcolm." Ignoring his protest, she breezed on by him with the table in hand.

Stubborn woman. Stubborn and strong and capable. She wasn't a woman afraid to get her hands dirty and do real work. Damn it, he didn't need more reasons to find Charlotte Vasquez appealing.

Once the trailer was unloaded and the pieces he'd brought had been put in place to her specifications, he turned a circle to take it in. Evidently, she'd finished unpacking everything onto the shelves while he'd been gone, and he was forced to admit she'd been right. Even without the sofa and some of the other big pieces, he got a sense of the inviting vibe she'd been going for.

"It looks nice."

She popped him on the arm with the back of her hand. "See? I told you. Cozy." Her sunshiny smile hit him right in the solar plexus, and he felt the corner of his mouth lifting in response.

Because he was struck by the urge to kiss her again, he began to gather broken-down boxes to throw in the back of the 4x4. "We should go get another load." He'd have preferred to wait for Connor or Raleigh, but he knew Charlotte was going to argue. They'd figure it out.

"Can we swing by number eight on the way? I want to see

what kind of shape it's in, so I can start making notes about supplies and figuring out the plan for renovation."

"Aye."

They finished loading the trash, then Charlotte locked up and climbed into the passenger seat for the short drive to the next cottage on their list.

Malcolm could tell right off, there was more roof work to be done. A tree branch had fallen on one end at some point, breaking quite a few of the slate tiles. There'd likely be water damage inside. The rest of the stone exterior seemed like it was in decent shape at first glance. Grabbing a torch, he headed for the door. It wasn't locked. There was nothing worth stealing in any of these places. The hinges squeaked as he shoved it open.

Charlotte peered around him. "If this were a horror movie, bats would be flying out the door."

"It's no' outside the realm of possible. We've not disturbed anything yet."

"Seriously?" She leapt forward, hunching against his back, so his body was a shield between her and the door.

He couldn't quite bring himself to shake her hands off his waist as he eased inside. Panning the light around the ceiling, he quickly confirmed they were alone. "No wee flying beasties."

"But maybe a two-legged one. Are those signs of a recent fire?" Not waiting for his reply, she skirted past him.

Malcolm swung the light over to what she'd picked out with her cell phone flashlight. A small pile of partly burned wood lay beneath the hole in the roof. There was evidence of smoke on the timbers above. "Someone's been here for certain."

They split apart, exploring the rest of the cottage. And in the back bedroom, they found a bundled sleeping bag.

"Someone's been staying here." Charlotte squatted to pick up something with a metallic gleam from the floor. "Energy bar wrappers. Same kind I found at the cottage we're finishing now."

"What? When?"

"Several weeks ago, the day I demoed the original bathroom

wall. I didn't think anything of it. I figure you or someone else had dropped it when you were last working on the place."

On a day she'd been working alone. Malcolm didn't like it.

She straightened. "Do you think it's a hillwalker? Like the one Raleigh found this summer, who thought these cabins were bothies?"

"I dinna think so. Finding evidence of one, maybe. But two? Seems more likely we've got a squatter."

"What do we do about it? Call the police?"

"We can make a report, but they're going to need more evidence before they can do anything. It's no' like we have a suspect we can point them to."

"What if we could get them evidence?" Her tone made it very clear she had an idea.

"What do you have in mind?"

"We had an issue on the ranch several years back with some cattle thieves. The property was too big to install full security camera coverage everywhere, so we ended up putting out game cameras. You know, the kind that only turns on when there's motion detected? It wasn't fancy, but it did the trick, and they caught the guys who were behind it. Seems like something along those lines would be easy to set up here."

Malcolm nodded. "It's a good idea. I've got a few back at my flat that I use to monitor some of the wildlife from time to time."

"Then let's go get them. The sooner we get them set up, the more likely we are to catch whoever it is. He'll probably be back for his sleeping bag."

"It's a solid plan. I don't want you working on any of the cottages by yourself until this is resolved."

The voice that had been so warm and easy with him all afternoon chilled. "I beg your pardon?"

"We dinna ken who's behind this. No' what they want or why they're here."

She crossed her arms, her jaw taking on a stubborn cast. "Malcolm, nobody is out to get me. I've been working on these cottages for months now with no problem. We've got too much to do for me to be hamstrung on work now, and you've got too many other responsibilities to babysit me."

Struggling to find some calm when his own temper was roused, Malcolm managed to keep his voice even. "I dinna expect it'll take too long to get an answer. Until then, I'm asking you to humor me. Please. I want you safe. Promise me, Charlotte."

The belligerent set to her jaw eased a fraction at his use of her name. She heaved a massive sigh. "Fine. I promise. For now."

Recognizing that was as good as it was going to get, he gestured toward the door. "Then let's go get those cameras."

Six

By the time they finished installing cameras, Malcolm had to go see to something or other on the estate, which meant Charlotte was on her own, forbidden from doing more work on the cottages. At least, for now.

That whole situation irked her. She hated being told what to do. Especially by a grumpy, dictatorial man. But he'd asked her not to. Sort of. He'd actually said, "Please," a word she hadn't thought was in his vocabulary.

"He wants me safe. What does that even mean?"

Bubbles bounced into her lap. "Baaa!"

"I know! It's confusing. He's confusing. Is he just spouting general good sense and trying to avoid liability because he's the estate manager? Or is it something else?"

"Baaaaaaaaa!" Buttercup insisted.

"Baaa baaaa!" Blossom argued, little tail wagging.

"I swear, it was easier when he was just being a grump. When he didn't care, I could just act however I wanted around him because it didn't matter. He was going to be who he is, no matter what. But something's... shifted, and now I feel all... squirrelly inside." The inconvenient attraction she felt suddenly seemed like more somehow, and the question of whether he actually returned that attraction had been driving her crazy.

"Baaa?" Buttercup butted her head against Charlotte's arm and peered up with those big, liquid eyes.

"Okay, okay. Enough about my problems. You're ready for your close-up." Shifting to her knees, she set Bubbles on her feet and pulled out her phone, swiping open the camera and turning it to video. "Okay, girls, get your cute on!"

By the time she'd finished playing with the babies and uploading another video to social media, Charlotte hadn't worked off much of the restlessness. Her next best fallback was cooking. Instead of heading up to the manor house to take advantage of the larger kitchen, she elected to stick to something simple that she could prepare in the smaller one in her flat. Enchiladas would be easy enough and would keep until whenever Malcolm got home. She lost herself in the familiar rhythm of the kitchen, soaking in the spicy scents of home as she made the sauce from scratch and assembled the casserole. As a rule, she loved feeding people because food was about so much more than the stomach. It fed the soul. If anyone needed his soul fed, it was Malcolm Niall.

The timer was just about to go off when she heard his door shut. What was it with that man not knowing how to close a door quietly? Whatever. It was in her favor tonight. Switching the oven off, she went to knock on his door.

He hadn't even shed his fleece when he answered.

"Bring the computer with the camera feeds over to my place."

His brows drew together. "What?"

"We both agreed that whoever this is will probably be coming back tonight, at least to get their stuff, if not to stay another night. That means a stakeout to watch the camera feeds. Why shouldn't we be well fed and comfortable while we watch?"

"We?"

"Don't think you're going to be doing this without me.

Come on." Without waiting to see if he followed, she went back to her flat, leaving the door open.

When his boots sounded on the stoop, she counted it as a win. Her door he shut without slamming, so maybe he could be taught. Hearing no further movement, Charlotte turned to find him standing agape at the entrance, staring at her space. She realized this was the first time he'd been in her apartment.

It was more or less a mirror image of his, but she didn't think it could be any more different. Where his flat was spartan and minimalist, hers was a riot of texture and color. When Raleigh had offered her the space, he'd told her to grab any extra furniture pieces she wanted from the manor house to make her place more comfortable, and she'd taken him at his word. On top of the eclectic mix of furniture, she'd been adding her own touches as her family continued to slowly ship her things from Texas. Patterned pillows and throws added pops of brightness to the otherwise drab interior, and an assortment of potted plants added life. There were bowls of pretty stones, books about every subject under the sun, and dozens of framed photos of friends and family.

"When did you put all of this in here?"

"Over the past couple months. As I've said before, I like making spaces comfortable. Please sit. The food is just about ready."

"You're really moving in."

She paused as she pulled plates out of the cabinets. "I am. Did you think my being here was temporary?" Did he hope it was? The idea of that caused a pit in Charlotte's stomach.

"I hadn't thought about it. This is…"

"A lot?"

"Homey."

She couldn't decide if he thought that was a good thing or not. He clearly had a complicated relationship with the idea of home, after his mom walking out on him as a child, then losing his daughter and wife. Even Afton. It seemed most of the people he'd cared about had left him in one way or another. After all that, Charlotte could admit he'd earned the right to his grumpi-tude. But that hadn't stopped her from trying to lighten that habitual dour mood. She'd coaxed a few almost smiles out of him over the past couple of weeks and considered it a victory. Maybe tonight she'd coax out more.

"Go ahead and set up the computer. I'll dish this up."

She flitted around her kitchen, plating up enchiladas and topping them with sour cream. She even added a sprig of fresh cilantro from her potted herbs to each plate for garnish. Eating began with the eyes, after all.

Malcolm looked up from the laptop as she brought over the food. His eyes widened, his nostrils flaring. "What's that?"

"Beef enchiladas. My mom's recipe. Or as close as I can get with the ingredients over here. I had my sister send me spices by the case."

He accepted a plate and brought it to his nose, closing his eyes and inhaling. "This smells amazing."

"We aren't afraid of spice where I come from. They aren't set-your-mouth-on-fire hot, but I didn't think about dialing back the heat."

"Good. I like some heat."

She'd have sworn something flashed in his hazel eyes, there, then gone again as fast as she could blink.

Heat flushed her cheeks for reasons she didn't want to think about as she sat next to him on the sofa. Because it was easier than looking at Malcolm, she fixed her gaze on the cluster of static images on the laptop screen. The three cameras caught almost every angle of the cottage, and she could only hope that their squatter hadn't been around to see the two of them hiding each one.

Silence settled but for the scrape of utensils against plates and the occasional low groan of pleasure from her companion. If nothing else, she could tell he absolutely liked her cooking. It was a skill she took pride in. But she couldn't quite remember the last time she'd been jealous that it was her food and not her eliciting that kind of noise from a man.

For just a moment, she considered asking him straight out whether she was reading the situation correctly. But then she remembered that horrible morning after, when his relief that nothing had happened between them had been so profound, and he'd insisted she was the last woman he needed to get tangled up with. Whatever apologies he'd made hadn't been about that. They'd been about her need to mother people. Better to keep quiet and assume she was in this alone.

Malcolm ate every bite, and she thought he might even lick the plate. His gaze slid over to the kitchen counter. "That was pure dead brilliant. Is there more?"

Charlotte laughed, pleased. "Of course. Mama always said the way to a man's heart was through his stomach."

When he only blinked at her, she played the words back in her head and winced. "Not that I'm trying to seduce you with food. It's just she made all her recipes with Papi in mind, and he could eat a lot and—I'll just get you some more."

Leaping to her feet, she snatched his plate and hurried to the kitchen, cheeks flaming. God, why couldn't the floor just open up and swallow her?

As she scooped another couple of enchiladas onto his plate, her mouth opened and more words fell out. "I'm making sopapillas for dessert." She hadn't actually planned on making dessert, but her feet carried her to the cabinet, and she began to pull out ingredients. "Have you ever had sopapillas? They're a sort of fried pastry that's finished off with a sprinkle of cinnamon and drizzled with honey. Will you have room for dessert after another serving of these?"

The enchiladas. Right, I haven't given him those yet.

She turned to reach for his plate again and walked right into Malcolm, hard enough that she bounced off that broad chest. As they had earlier in the day, those big, work-roughened hands cupped her elbows to steady her. How the hell had he made it across the kitchen without her hearing?

He stared down at her in consternation, his expression serious. Because he was always serious. "Woman, do you ever stop talking?"

Not when I'm mortified, I don't.

"I'm sorry. I really wasn't trying to flirt and make this weird. That's not what I—"

He closed the distance between them, pressing his mouth to hers in a fleeting kiss that dried up the river of words.

Wide-eyed, she stared up at him when he pulled back.

Those thick brows of his drew together. "Hush."

Charlotte didn't think she could have found a single word in that moment if her life depended on it.

Evidently satisfied with her silence, he lifted her to her toes and bent his head again, settling his lips over hers. The man kissed like he did everything else—with studied deliberation and intensity. And Charlotte was a hundred percent on board with it. She twined her arms around those broad shoulders she'd wanted to get her hands on for months and drew him closer for a deeper kiss. On a growl, he wrapped one big arm around her waist and hoisted her higher, devouring her mouth the same way he'd devoured her food. His easy ability to manhandle her was such an incredible turn on. As was the growing evidence of his arousal pressing against her belly.

Wanting to feel the press of it between her thighs, she tightened her hold, about to lift her legs to wrap around his waist, when some odd chime penetrated her haze of lust.

Malcolm's head came up. His expression was dialed to fierce and hungry, and all she could think was *Oh, yes, more.*

But he apparently didn't get the memo because he let her go and walked across the room.

Charlotte swayed where she stood, having to work extra hard to convince her legs to hold her up.

"Gotcha."

Her brain hadn't managed to come back online to process what had just happened. "What?"

Malcolm grabbed his keys. "Our squatter has arrived. Get your coat."

Coat? There was so much heat pumping off her right now, she could power the entire village.

When he just stood there, staring expectantly, waiting for her to get her ass in gear, she shook off the remaining dizziness. "Right."

Recognizing that they definitely weren't going to address that kiss that had all but incinerated her underwear, she grabbed her coat as ordered and followed him out the door.

***

Malcolm hadn't meant to kiss her. He'd just wanted to ease that painful embarrassment, or maybe mention he'd be completely fine with her seducing him with food. She was one hell of a cook. But she wouldn't stop talking long enough for him to get a word in edge-wise. A kiss had seemed the quickest way to interrupt the babble.

And then... Then he hadn't been able to stop himself from leaning in again, pulled to her unapologetic warmth like a magnet pointing to true north. He didn't trust it. Didn't believe he deserved it. But apparently, he wasn't immune. And, damn it, now that he had the taste of her, once would never be enough. A simple kiss wouldn't be enough.

Not that there'd been anything simple about that kiss. If the camera alert hadn't sounded, he'd have been searching for the nearest empty counter to get his hands on more of her, and he was pretty sure she'd have let him. If they'd gotten to that point, where would they have stopped? *Would* they have stopped? It seemed all that sniping antagonism had morphed into the kind of heat that only ended one way—naked and sated.

Except they hadn't gotten that far, and now she sat in the

passenger seat, staring resolutely ahead, kiss-swollen lips pressed into a line. He never would have imagined he'd *miss* her incessant talking. At least when she did that, he knew where they stood. This silent Charlotte worried him. She hadn't said a single word since they got into the 4x4.

Maybe it was a good thing they'd been interrupted. Getting involved with her beyond their reluctant partnership on the cottage renovations was probably a mistake. Nothing good could come of getting more entangled with her. Not for her, at least. She was legitimately starting a new life here. She deserved better than the likes of him.

Just shy of the curve in the road that led to the cottage, Malcolm rolled to a stop and cut the lights. They were far enough from the house that their intruder shouldn't have heard the engine. Now that they were here, he was regretting his automatic invitation. They had no idea who or what they'd find, and he was the dumbass who'd inadvertently put her in potential harm's way.

"You should wait here."

Charlotte merely fixed him with a withering stare. Was that about his request or the fact that he hadn't said anything on the drive about the kiss, either?

Biting back his frustration, he released the seatbelt. "Fine. But stay behind me." He could at least put himself between her and whatever prospective danger lurked ahead.

Malcolm grabbed the tranquilizer gun from the rack in the back, and they slid out of the vehicle, closing their doors with a quiet click. He had plenty of practice walking silently through the woods because of all his years as a hunting guide. He expected Charlotte to crunch her way through the leaves, as most people did when they were trying to be quiet. But again, she surprised him. She moved with almost as much stealth as he. In truth, he likely only won out because of his familiarity with the land.

As they neared the cottage, Malcolm spotted the faint glow of a light through the window. It didn't waver, and he scented no smoke, so he was banking on an electric torch. There was no good way to peek inside without giving themselves away, so he'd have to rely on the element of surprise. These little cabins had only one door in or out. This one had a couple of broken windows, but they were narrow and would be difficult for a grown man to shimmy through.

Leaning close, he pressed his mouth to Charlotte's ear. "I'm going inside. Stay out here in case he gets past me."

He caught her shudder as he eased back to assess her agreement. There was no reading her expression in the dark, but she held up a sturdy branch she'd picked up somewhere along the way. It wouldn't do a hell of a lot in the face of a gun or knife, so he'd just have to make sure their interloper didn't give him the slip. But at least she was armed with something.

With a nod, he crept closer. The tranq gun he carried wasn't actually loaded, but he was banking on the squatter not being aware of that. The night was chill, so perhaps they'd luck out and the guy would already be in his sleeping bag, conveniently immobilized. In his head, Malcolm counted the steps from the entrance to the back bedroom, where he suspected the intruder was hiding. The door to that room opened inward, to the left. He'd come in low and use that for cover if needed.

Looking back once to check Charlotte's position at the treeline, he braced himself and burst inside. The door banged back against the wall, and Malcolm charged toward the back bedroom. That door was ajar, and he caught a flurry of movement. He burst inside, his gaze going to the puddle of fabric on the floor, before snapping up to see a slim figure disappearing through the window.

"Oy! Stop!"

Malcolm lunged, but the figure disappeared into the black. Swearing, he reversed directions, racing back toward the front door. From somewhere behind the house, he heard an *oof* and a thump.

Charlotte.

He skirted the edge of the cottage, prepared to use the butt of the tranq gun as a bludgeon as necessary.

But it was Charlotte on her feet, the branch braced against her shoulder like a bat, waiting for another swing. "Stay down."

The figure on the ground continued to wheeze.

"You okay?" Malcolm asked.

"Better than he is. He basically clothes-lined himself. I think he just had the breath knocked out of him."

Shifting his grip on the gun, Malcolm strode closer and pulled out the torch he'd shoved into a pocket. "Let's see who we've got here." He snapped on the light and shone it on their captive.

Charlotte gasped, and he froze.

Their squatter wasn't a man at all. It was a skinny, hollow-cheeked boy, who looked absolutely scared to death.

SEVEN

A child. Their intruder was *a child*. Charlotte pegged him as no more than thirteen, though it was a little hard to tell in the flashlight's glare. He was skinny and dirty, with the kind of sharp angles in his face that only came with hunger.

Horrified, she tossed the branch away. "Oh, my God. Are you okay? Did I hurt you?"

As the boy still hadn't caught his breath, he didn't answer.

Malcolm shifted the light so it wasn't shining in his eyes and took a step forward. The kid curled in on himself as if bracing for a blow.

Every maternal instinct she had flared to life. She didn't for a moment believe that Malcolm would strike a child, but she wouldn't put it past him to use his size to intimidate. He wasn't exactly the cuddly sort.

Instead, he offered a hand to help the boy up.

The kid didn't move.

Malcolm lowered to one knee, folding his hands. "You're no' in trouble, lad. Have you eaten?"

So he hadn't missed that, either.

Confusion flickered over the child's pale face, but he shook his head slowly.

Whatever else was going on in this boy's life, this Charlotte could fix. "Let's take him home."

He scrambled back. "No!"

She held up her empty hands. "Wait! Wait! Ours. We'll get you a hot meal and get you warmed up."

The kid split a look between the two of them, as if trying to assess his chances of getting away, versus how serious they were about the food.

Hoping to put him more at ease, she pressed a hand to her chest. "I'm Charlotte Vasquez. This is Malcolm Niall. What's your name, darlin'?"

He swallowed. "G... Gavin."

No last name. That would take some time to wrangle out of him.

"Well, Gavin, I'm sorry about the misunderstanding. We thought you were a burglar."

Insult whipped color into Gavin's face. "I'm no thief!"

Though a million and one questions scrolled through her mind about how long he'd been out here and what he'd been living on, she simply nodded. "Of course not. So you'll come with us and let us give you some supper as an apology. All right?"

When he still looked uncertain, Malcolm quietly added, "You can't stay here, lad. Best come with us."

He offered his hand again, and this time, Gavin took it. Malcolm tugged him upright, and it became readily apparent that the boy was already taller than her. Not that it was a high bar.

Because she was afraid he might still pull a runner, Charlotte companionably slipped her arm through his. "Have you ever had Tex-Mex food, Gavin?"

He glanced down at their joined arms and dark hair flopped into his face. "Uh... no."

"Then you're in for a treat. That's my specialty. I'm from Texas, you see, and I made enchiladas for supper."

"What are enchiladas?"

"They're delicious, is what they are," Malcolm put in.

Charlotte flashed him a smile. She kept up a running commentary all through the walk to the 4x4 and the drive back to her flat, describing the dish and the ingredients. When he didn't hesitate to follow them inside, she knew she'd hooked him with the prospect of food. His nose twitched as he stepped through the door, his eyes going wide.

"Make yourself at home and wash your hands. I'll get these warmed up for you."

The plate of Malcolm's seconds lay abandoned on the counter. For a few fleeting moments, she flashed back to the kiss that had distracted her from serving them. Heat flashed through her system at the memory, and her lips tingled with yearning for more.

So not the time. Get it together, girl.

Plating up three of the remaining enchiladas, she popped them into the microwave.

"Do you drink milk?"

Gavin made a face.

"It'll help temper the heat, in case they're a little too spicy for you." And it would get some more calories in him.

"Oh. Okay."

She poured him a glass. "It's from cows here on the estate. Probably the closest you've ever come to meeting your food." If he was from one of the other rural farms in the area, surely he'd correct her.

When he said nothing, she simply added a dollop of sour cream to the top of the reheated enchiladas and placed them on the table in front of him. For half a second, she thought he might forego the utensils and fall on the food like a starving animal. Then he picked up the fork and cut a huge bite, shoving it into his mouth without ceremony. Brown eyes went wide.

"Oh my God." At least, that's what Charlotte thought he said around the food. Table manners were way on down her list of things that needed dealing with just now.

"Fair brilliant, aye?" Malcolm prompted, sliding into a chair.

Gavin's answer was to start inhaling everything on his plate.

Charlotte laid a soft hand on the boy's shoulder, confirming the bony feel of him beneath the jacket that was far too light for the cold nights they'd been having. "Don't choke. There's more, if you want it." Her gaze shifted to Malcolm's over his head. "Do you want the rest of yours?"

"Please."

There was that word again.

As she warmed up his second helping, Charlotte noticed how Malcolm seemed to be trying to minimize his size. Not an easy feat, considering he was over six feet tall. But she approved of how he was trying to *not* be intimidating to the child. Hopefully, they'd get more out of him like that.

By the time she set Malcolm's rewarmed plate in front of him, Gavin had finished his first round and looked at her with Oliver eyes. With an encouraging smile, she set about plating the last two enchiladas and did a mental inventory of her food stores, trying to think what else she could prepare quickly if he was still hungry.

Malcolm forked up a bite. "How long have you been out there, lad?" He posed the question easily, as if they were just having a conversation.

Gavin's expression turned wary.

This time it was Charlotte who offered reassurances, along with more food. "You're not in trouble, sweetheart."

His fingers worked at a loose thread on the cuff of his jacket. "Nearly six weeks."

Charlotte pressed her lips together to keep from crying out. *Six weeks?* This boy had been out on his own for more than a month? The idea of it hurt her, and given his initial reaction to Malcolm, she could only imagine what he was running from.

Malcolm nodded. "Impressive. We only figured out someone was about today. You've been moving around, using the cottages for shelter?"

"Y... yes, sir. I didnae break anything. I swear!"

"Nobody said you did. The only reason we knew at all was

because we found your sleeping bag. What have you been doing with yourself during the day?"

"Fishing, mostly."

So that's how he'd kept himself fed. Between the nearby loch and the streams that fed it, there were plenty of opportunities. And until the past couple of weeks, the weather had been relatively mild. But it had turned downright cold with the imminent arrival of November.

"You're no' from Glenlaig, are you?"

Gavin shook his head.

Malcolm cut into his last enchilada. "I didnae think so. If you'd been gone that long from here, I'd have heard about it by now."

"Nobody's looking for me."

Charlotte slid into the next chair at the table. "How do you know?"

"My ma's gone. My da's not usually sober enough to notice if I'm there or no'."

Beneath the table, she fisted her hand as outrage bloomed. No one should treat a child with that kind of disregard.

Malcolm kept his tone even. "Who's your da?"

Fresh fear flickered across Gavin's face.

"I'll no' be telling him you're here, either way."

After a long pause, Gavin finally whispered, "Simon Elliot."

Legitimate shock momentarily blanked Malcolm's face. Evidently, the name meant something to him. "You came all the way here from Duntyre?"

Charlotte tried to place the town, but there were so many little villages in the Highlands, she hadn't learned more than those in the immediate area.

"Aye. It's no' so far as the crow flies."

"A good thirty miles." He scrubbed a hand over his face. "Simon Elliot."

Charlotte needed more information. "You know his father?"

"In a manner of speaking." It was clear he knew more than he was saying. Judging by the battle light in his eyes, none of it was good. "We'll abso-fucking-lutely not be telling him Gavin is here." The matter-of-fact pronouncement seemed to relax the boy even further.

He laid his fork down on a plate that had been all but licked clean. "What will you do wi' me?"

"I dinna ken yet. But sending you home isnae on the table. For tonight, you'll stay with one of us. We'll figure out a plan tomorrow, after breakfast."

"Stay here?" Gavin asked.

"You'd rather have a warm bed than the hard ground and a sleeping bag, wouldn't you?" Charlotte prompted. "I've got a spare bed upstairs with your name on it. And fresh biscuits in the morning."

Amusement cut through some of the lingering fear. "Biscuits? For breakfast?"

"Right. What we call biscuits and what y'all call biscuits aren't the same thing. In America, biscuits are a breakfast food. You'll find out in the morning." By her estimation, Gavin was right at what she thought of as the hollow leg years, when he'd have a hard time eating enough to keep up with the growth spurts. And there was no guarantee he'd had enough food even before he'd been out on his own. She'd see to that, so long as he was here. "C'mon. I'll show you to your room."

She led Gavin upstairs, giving him a quick tour of the guest room and the hall bath. "And here's a fresh towel, if you'd like to shower before bed."

The boy stood there, brown eyes beginning to gleam, chin quivering with emotion. "Thank you."

Unable to stop herself, Charlotte laid both hands on his thin shoulders. When he didn't flinch away, she called it a victory. "We may not know what to do with you yet, but we won't send you back to a bad situation. Okay?"

He swallowed and nodded.

"Get a shower and some rest. I expect it's been a while since you've had either. We'll see you in the morning."

Downstairs, Malcolm had started on the dishes.

"So, how bad is his dad, really?"

He turned from the sink, expression grave. "Bad. I knew him from years ago. He was bad then, and I can only presume he's worse now. I didnae know he had a child. I won't let him go back there."

Charlotte hadn't expected this softer, gentler side of him. Now wasn't the time to think about how very much she liked it. "So, what are we going to do?"

"We'll check on things tomorrow. I can make some discreet inquiries. In the meantime, I'm sleeping on the sofa."

"The sofa? Why? You don't fit."

"In case he tries to sneak out in the middle of the night. He needs help, but he has to stick around so we can do it."

She appreciated that he automatically included her in that "we".

"I'll get you a pillow and blanket."

———

The squeak of a stair had Malcolm shooting upright in the pale gray light just before dawn. The sudden motion had him biting back a string of curses as his back made its profound objections to his sleeping arrangements known. He'd definitely need to visit the chiropractor the next village over to recover.

"Sorry!" Charlotte whispered. "I didn't mean to wake you." She stood at the base of the stairs, still on her tiptoes.

He sucked in a breath and scrubbed both hands over his face. "S'fine."

She switched on the light over the stove, and he could see she was already fully dressed, but for her shoes. As she sat at the kitchen table to tug on her boots, her long, thick hair swung forward, obscuring her face, and he couldn't help but think of another morning, after a very different night. How differently that could have gone if he hadn't been an asshole. Fresh shame trickled through him at the memory, tying his tongue.

Charlotte straightened, tucking that hair behind her ear. "I'm gonna go feed the babies, but I'll be back in a little bit to start on the biscuits. There are eggs and bacon, if Gavin wakes up before I get back. And of course, there's coffee."

Malcolm nodded. "I can see to that."

"Okay. I'll be back."

She stepped out into the dawn, leaving him feeling creaky and ill at ease. Given the position of the rising sun, he'd have his own chores to do. But Raleigh had taken over some of the feeding of the stock since he arrived, his lifetime as a rancher conditioning him to early rising and farm chores, so Malcolm had a little time, yet. He had no idea what he was going to tell his boss about Gavin. That would depend on the boy himself and whether he accepted the offer Malcolm had come up with during the hours of discomfort on the too-short sofa, and on the results of the inquiries still to be made.

For the moment, the only answer he was interested in was coffee. He blessed Charlotte several times over for her fussy taste in it. She had the good beans and a French press that made for a rich, nuanced cup. Malcolm didn't bother with such things for himself. The caffeine was the important part, and he was usually intent on getting moving as quickly as possible, but he appreciated the difference when he tasted it. He'd just put the top on the press when that squeaky stair alerted him to Gavin's presence.

"Morning."

At the lack of response, Malcolm turned to find him standing at the base of the stairs, backpack over one shoulder.

"Going somewhere?"

"No." The deepening guilt on his face said otherwise.

"Have a seat. I was about to start breakfast. How do you like your eggs?"

"I dinna ken. Scrambled?"

"All right. You want bacon?"

"Sure."

The kid sat, placing the backpack at his feet. Malcolm kept his attention on the food prep, giving the boy a chance to relax. Once the bacon was frying, he turned to face Gavin. "Well, I've given it some thought. I want to offer you a job."

"What?" If he'd just told the kid he was secret royalty, he didn't think Gavin would've looked more surprised.

"It'd be pretty physical work. Helping with livestock as needed. Learning to do repairs on fencing. Some renovations on those cottages you were staying in. It'll depend on what comes up. I'm the estate manager for Lochmara, so my duties are varied, and I need help with different things by the day. In exchange, I'm offering a fair hourly wage and room and board. A proper place for you to stay, so you're not having to sneak around."

The surprise melted into suspicion. "Why?"

Malcolm shrugged. "I can use the help. And I've met your dad." He cracked eggs into a bowl, wishing they were Simon Elliot's skull. "Sometimes a man just needs a hand out of a bad situation."

He'd had plenty of time last night to remember how Peter Lennox had helped drag him out of the bottle all those years ago. If Malcolm could pay it forward with this kid, he would.

Gavin picked at the corner of a placemat. "I guess we could try it. What about your wife?"

"My what? I don't have a wife."

"Girlfriend, then. Charlotte."

Well, damn if that didn't send Malcolm's brain on a merry little trip into fantasy land. It was way easier than it should've been to imagine his life merged with hers, with all the freedom in the world to pursue more of those passionate kisses and beyond. As things stirred below his belt, he cleared his throat. "She's not my wife. Not my girlfriend, either."

Gavin frowned. "But don't you live here?"

"No, I live next door."

"Then why are you here so early?"

"To cook you breakfast." That seemed a better answer than the truth.

The front door opened, and Charlotte came in with a gust of wind. "It's brisk this morning. The triplets are extra perky. Morning, Gavin."

"Triplets? You have kids?"

She laughed. "Lambs. Here, I just took some video of them for their Instagram account."

Gavin perked up at the sight of the lambs' latest antics, and the sharing of them clearly gave Charlotte lots of joy. Her smile radiated, brightening the dim space. Of course, that got Malcolm thinking about the kiss they still hadn't talked about. With all her focus on the boy, now definitely wasn't the time. That was as it should be. She was good with him. Comfortable and friendly. He supposed she would be since she'd more or less raised Raleigh from a pretty similar age. Based on the stars in Gavin's eyes, it was pretty clear he was already nursing a crush on her. Kindness and a pretty smile would go a long way.

"There was talk of biscuits last night," Malcolm reminded her.

"So there was." She put her phone away and began pulling out ingredients. "I see there's already bacon."

"And eggs ready to go on." He added two more for her.

As she pulled together the dough, he figured he better bring her in on the plan.

"Gavin will be staying."

"Oh?"

"He's taking a job on the estate." Malcolm knew there were a hundred details to figure out. Like where the kid would permanently sleep. He couldn't very well volunteer Charlotte's guest room for that purpose without having consulted her.

But she didn't point out any of the hurdles they needed to jump. She simply nodded. "Okay. Then we should retrieve the rest of your stuff."

Gavin's ears turned red as he laid a protective hand over his bag. "This is everything."

They both looked at the one small backpack.

By this point, Malcolm had learned to read Charlotte. Not that it was that difficult. It was clear the boy's circumstances broke that big heart of hers. But she said nothing to embarrass him.

"Then you'll need a few more things. We'll go into town to pick some up."

Gavin balked, obviously reluctant to leave the estate, no doubt wanting to avoid being spotted by anyone who could report back to his father.

Charlotte just kept talking. "I need some things from Inverness, anyway. That ought to make a pretty reasonable shopping option. More choices there."

And it was more than two hours in the opposite direction from Duntyre.

Well, played.

"Malcolm, what do you have to finish today so you can go with us?"

And that was how he found himself recruited for a shopping day with his part-time nemesis and increasing obsession, and the boy it seemed they were informally adopting.

EIGHT

"It should be short."

Charlotte tried not to be distracted by the bulge of Malcolm's biceps as he loomed, arms folded, legs spread, as if he was ready to take the salon by storm. "It's Gavin's hair. The length and cut is his choice."

For his part, Gavin sat in the stylist's chair, looking amused that the two of them were arguing about such a thing. The one point they agreed on was that he needed some kind of haircut. His dark brown hair was shaggy and unkempt, long enough to pull into a stubby tail. He hadn't had any kind of cut or shaping in more than a year.

The stylist, a twenty-something woman with a stud in her nose and purple streaks in her own brunette hair, watched the byplay for a few more moments before turning to him. "Are your parents always this opinionated about hair?"

Charlotte and Malcolm turned as one. "We're not his parents."

Gavin shrugged. "Long story."

The woman nodded. "Right. Well, what is it you want, lad?"

"I dinna ken. It's hair."

"Then how about we split the difference, and I give you a cut that'll keep awhile and flatter the shape of your face?"

"That sounds perfect. We'll be right over here." Charlotte grabbed Malcolm's arm and towed him over to the waiting area so he wasn't crowding the poor stylist.

He growled a little as he sat. "A short, clean cut makes him less recognizable," he murmured.

"We've got much bigger things to worry about than that. Have you heard anything back from your inquiries?"

"Not yet. Far as I can tell, no one's looking for him. Simon hasn't reported him missing. I dinna ken whether that's because he hasn't noticed or disnae care."

"Neither's a good situation."

"I'll no' see him go back into an abusive household." His stubbled jaw firmed, and a battle light brightened those hazel eyes.

Charlotte wanted to stroke the tension away. To kiss those firm lips again. Instead, she squeezed his arm. "Neither will I. But this is more complicated than just giving him a job and a place to stay and buying him some new clothes. I have no idea how child welfare laws are set up in this country, but I feel certain we're probably violating some of them."

He glared. "You're no' saying we should just turn him over?"

"No. We need more information. That's gonna take time. I think we keep him hidden, keep him safe, while we acquire it. See what our options are and how it goes with him. Right now, he's rolling along with all this, but that doesn't mean he actually trusts us. Why should he? We're still relative strangers."

"Strangers who've given more of a damn about him in twenty-four hours than his own blood has in maybe ever."

Charlotte met his gaze. "Strangers who will keep giving a damn because it's the right thing to do."

His big hand settled over hers, where she still gripped his arm, and he nodded.

For all that they argued and disagreed on a multitude of

things, she understood that, in this, they were united. They'd work together to see that Gavin was safe, no matter what.

He glanced back toward the boy. "What's Raleigh going to say about all this?"

"I have no idea. But he'll no more want to return Gavin to a bad situation than we do. You leave him to me."

By the time Gavin rose from the stylist's chair twenty minutes later, he did, indeed, look like an entirely different kid. Charlotte nodded in satisfaction. "Excellent. And now, I think we could all do with some lunch. Gavin, what would you like?"

His thin shoulders twitched. "Anything's fine."

Figuring he was a child who'd never gotten a chance to actually *be* a child, she tried to think about what he probably never got to eat. "Pizza?"

His face brightened. "I like pizza."

They found a little Italian eatery that did stone-fired crust and ordered the biggest pie they had. As with dinner last night and breakfast this morning, Gavin dove in, inhaling two slices before she'd even gotten through half of one. She wondered if he was still legitimately hungry or if he was afraid the food would disappear. That this whole situation wasn't going to last. It was probably a little of both.

She waited until he'd scarfed down his fourth slice before bringing up the elephant no one else was going to ask about. "So, one of the practicalities we need to consider is school."

Gavin stopped chewing, his jaw taking on a stubborn cast that seriously resembled Malcolm. "I'm no' going back."

Ignoring that, she gently pushed. "Would your dad think to look for you in school in Glenlaig?"

"I don't know. I doubt he thinks to look for me anywhere unless he wants a fresh punching bag."

At Malcolm's growl, she automatically reached out and laid a hand over his, but she kept her focus on the boy. "I have no idea what the school laws are in Scotland, but I'm certain you're of an age that you're required to be there. Now, we've already promised we're not going to do anything to put you in the path of danger, but we want to do this as much on the up and up as we can. That might mean online classes. But you'll have to do something, along with the duties Malcolm assigns you as his assistant. I'll look into it and see what would be required to get you enrolled."

Malcolm studied him. "You've not been in school since you left Duntyre, aye?"

"No."

"After more than a month out, with no' much more than a month to go in term, it makes more sense for him to start back in January. That gives us time to sort... everything else."

Gavin immediately jumped on board. "January sounds good."

Charlotte couldn't argue with the sense of that. "Fine. But know that's coming down the pike. Schooling is important."

His eyes dropped, and he began to pick at a pepperoni. "It disnae matter. You might decide no' to keep me by then."

Heart twisting, she met Malcolm's gaze. The kid needed some serious reassurance.

He leaned forward. "Gavin." He waited until the boy looked up. "We're no' going to force you into anything. If you decide you're no' happy wi' us, we'll help you find somewhere else. Will there be work and rules? Aye. They're part of life. They teach responsibility and respect. But in exchange, you'll have a place of your own, a roof over your head, and food in your belly. We willnae be kicking you out. Understand?"

His brown eyes glimmered, and his Adam's apple bobbed, so he simply nodded.

"All right. Finish your pizza. We've got a few more stops before we head home."

That was news to Charlotte. They'd already picked up everything on her list. "We do?"

"Aye. I thought we'd stop at some charity shops to see if we could find some furniture and things for his room."

They hadn't actually discussed *where* Gavin would be staying. She'd just kind of assumed he'd take her guest room.

"My room?"

"Charlotte's guest room is fine and all, but I've a spare room with nothing in it. We'll wrangle a bed from elsewhere on the estate, but this way, you'll be able to start from scratch. Make it your own."

Gavin looked stunned. "Truly?"

"A boy needs his own space."

Having raised Raleigh from a teenager, Charlotte knew this to be true. When Gavin rose to go refill his drink, she leaned toward Malcolm. "Are you okay having him living with you?"

"I'm the one who made the decision he should stay. I should be fully responsible."

She laid a hand on his arm. "We're in this together, Niall."

As their gazes locked, he settled his palm over hers again, warmth soaking into her. In that moment, they felt connected by a bigger purpose, and she wondered how the hell they'd ended up essentially co-parenting a teenage boy in less than a day when half the time they didn't even like each other all that much. But as he continued to stare at her, a different heat bloomed in her eyes. Yeah, he hadn't forgotten that kiss they'd yet to talk about either.

They'd deal with it, eventually. Right now, Gavin had to come first.

———

Leaving the boys to carry all their purchases up to Gavin's new room, Charlotte made her way up to the manor house. Their day in Inverness had stretched on a lot longer than she'd expected, putting them back after the usual dinner hour. She'd see about getting them all fed after she'd had a chance to speak to Raleigh. She wanted to get this part of things over with in case it turned out she was wrong about how he'd react to the situation.

At this time of night, he and Kyla were likely hanging out in the lounge, but given their newlywed status, she didn't just walk in. There was an unfortunate incident from Raleigh's teen years with a girl in a hayloft that she was in no hurry to repeat. Ever. After she'd given him a firm talking to about safe, consensual sex, and made sure he was fully supplied with condoms, they'd agreed never to speak of it again. And they hadn't.

Good Lord. If Gavin stuck around, did that mean she'd have to go through that awkward conversation again at some point?

Don't borrow trouble, woman.

Bracing herself, she knocked on the kitchen door. Loud enough they'd hear if they were downstairs, but quiet enough not to bother them if they were otherwise occupied. Luck was with her. Kyla answered the door a minute later, in flannel pajama pants and a sweatshirt, her long red hair twisted up and secured with a pen.

She beamed a welcoming smile. "Charlotte! What brings you by?"

"I was hoping to talk to your other half."

"Come on in. We're just watching a little TV."

Knowing how little downtime the two of them got between the running of both estates, she felt bad for interrupting. But this was important.

Raleigh rose from the sofa to give her a quick hug. "Hey! Wasn't expecting you tonight." He pulled back and searched her face. "Is everything okay?"

"Not exactly."

Kyla hovered by the door. "I can leave you two alone."

Charlotte was under no delusion that he'd keep what she was about to tell him a secret from his wife. "That's up to you. If you leave, you'll have plausible deniability."

Kyla and Raleigh exchanged a look, then Kyla resumed her seat on the couch beside her husband, taking his hand.

Charlotte appreciated the show of solidarity and loved seeing how close they'd become since they'd chosen to stay married, instead of divorcing after the marriage pact had been satisfied. Sometimes the Universe knew what it was doing. She could only hope that now was another of those times.

Raleigh braced his forearms on his knees and leaned forward. "What's going on, Charlotte?"

Over the course of the afternoon, she'd considered a hundred and one different ways to tell him. There was no graceful way to get into this. "So, Malcolm and I found a squatter in one of the cottages on the estate."

"Oh, was it another hiker?" Raleigh's face took on an edge of alarm. "Please tell me you didn't have some sort of situation where a body needed to be hidden."

She snorted an awkward laugh. "Nope. Not a body. A child."

He blinked, clearly waiting for the punchline. "I'm sorry. What?"

"The squatter is a thirteen-year-old boy. His name is Gavin. He made his way all the way here from Duntyre. On foot."

"So far," Kyla murmured.

Raleigh's golden-brown eyes sharpened as he processed all the potential implications. "Is he all right? Was he injured?"

"Thankfully, no. He's been on his own for about six weeks. A runaway. His mom's not in the picture. Dad's an abusive alcoholic. Malcolm knows something of the boy's father. None of it's good. We both feel strongly that he absolutely does not need to go back to where he came from. The truth is, if he gets sent back, he's just going to run away again, and who knows where he'll end up next time?" Winter was coming. If he tried to do the same thing again, he might freeze to death, or get hurt, or run into some kind of child predator...

Raleigh interrupted her train of disaster thoughts. "Okay, so what are we talking about here? Do you need help getting up with social services in Scotland or what?"

"Probably eventually. Right now, we want him to stay here. Malcolm has offered him a job helping out for room and board around the estate. We'll need to look into school at some point, but he's already been out for six weeks, and the term is going to be over in a few more, so that seems more like a problem for January, after we determine whether he's actually going to get to stay or not."

The pair of them stared at her long enough that Charlotte began to sweat.

A furrow appeared between Raleigh's brows, as if he were weighing his words. "So, let me get this straight. You've basically taken in a stray boy?"

"Yes, and no. He's actually going to be living with Malcolm."

"Malcolm? Mr. I'd-Be-Fine-Going-a-Month-Without-Human-Contact? Mr. Prefers-Animals-to-People? Are you sure about this? Don't get me wrong—he's a damned fine estate manager, but he's not exactly the paternal sort."

Charlotte thought of the unexpected gentleness he'd shown Gavin. There was far more beneath that gruff persona he presented to the world. "He might surprise you." He'd certainly surprised her. "Either way, we're on the same page about this."

"You and Malcolm?" he repeated, his tone ripe with disbelief.

"Yes, me and Malcolm." Annoyance began to prickle. They were getting away from the point.

"You'll have to excuse me if I'm having a little trouble wrapping my brain around the idea of you and Malcolm peacefully working together on anything."

"He did buy her sheep," Kyla pointed out, lips quirked in amusement.

"So he did," Raleigh conceded. "I can't imagine why."

Feeling a little defensive on Malcolm's behalf, Charlotte sighed. "They were an apology."

"For what?"

No way in hell was she telling him about that. He'd have a fit. "None of your business. We've sorted it. Anyway, believe me, I am every bit as surprised as you by the current turn of events, but we're in full agreement on this point. We want to help him. I know there are potentially some thorny legal issues around all of this, but we'd appreciate your discretion about the fact that the boy is here, and if you could put in a word with Hamish so we can actually get some legal advice on the situation, that would really help us out."

Kyla's blue eyes shone with sympathy. "Of course, we'll do that. You didn't need us to talk to Hamish."

"No, but it's on your property and under your nose, so this could blow back on y'all. If you've got any issue with us keeping this child here, now's the time to mention it so we can make other arrangements." She didn't have the foggiest idea what those arrangements might be, but she was hoping it wouldn't come to that.

"We don't want any kid to get put back in a bad situation," Raleigh assured her. "But are you sure you want to take on another unruly teenage boy?"

Relieved, she grinned and crossed over to pat his cheek. "Well, I think the first one turned out pretty well, so yes."

Kyla laughed. "I certainly can't argue with that. We're happy to do whatever's needed to rally the troops to keep the boy safe."

Charlotte let out a slow breath. "Thank you. Truly."

"We'll want to meet him at some point, when he's comfortable. And I'll want to talk to Malcolm about exactly what work he'll be doing. I'm sure there are liability issues to deal with."

"Gavin's a little skittish right now. But we'll see to all of that. Seriously, thank you for this. I know it's going to be potentially complicated, but it just feels like the right thing to do."

Raleigh rose and wrapped her in another tight hug. "That's always been your specialty. You let us know what you need."

She squeezed him and stepped back. "Now that you mention it, we're in search of another spare bed."

NINE

After twenty years of being a divorced bachelor, Malcolm was being forced out of his routine and comfort zone. It was his own damned fault. Charlotte had been more than willing for Gavin to stay with her. But he'd felt like the boy would be safer with him, should his father come looking. Not to mention, Charlotte. And a part of him had wanted to show Gavin that not all men were like Simon. Not that he'd had dealings with the other man in more than fifteen years, but he'd been a right shite before. Malcolm couldn't imagine he'd improved with age and single parenthood.

That the kid had agreed to the arrangement spoke of some measure of trust. Not a lot. Not yet. He was still scared that the rug would get yanked out from under him and he'd be out on his arse, so he hadn't stepped a toe out of line. Malcolm hoped there would come a time when Gavin felt comfortable enough to be messy and disrespectful, because it would mean he felt settled and safe. They'd deal with the ensuing annoyance of that when they got to it.

Because he was already looking at this for the long-haul, Malcolm was having to break out of some well-established personal ruts. Like occasionally conversing, and adopting an expression that wasn't a habitual scowl. His face actually *hurt* from the effort. But a week into having someone else in his space, it wasn't Gavin who'd made the biggest impact.

It was Charlotte.

She'd gracefully bent to the idea of the boy staying with Malcolm. She *hadn't* been willing to accept the minimalist decor he'd lived with for the past two decades, insisting that Gavin needed to feel like this was a home, not just a stopover. Not only had they fully furnished and kitted out the boy's room, but more furniture was finding its way into the rest of the flat. Art had made it onto the walls, including a selfie of the three of them she'd taken in Inverness that she'd had printed and framed. Pillows and throw blankets had materialized in the lounge. There was actual *color* in his space. She'd even brought in plants, for Chrissakes. Malcolm had agreed to take care of a person, not green things. When he'd confronted her about the fact that he already cared for thousands of acres of green, growing things, she'd simply said watering the plants would be one of Gavin's chores, something the lad had readily agreed to because he was absolutely smitten with her.

Malcolm couldn't blame him. She was warm and affectionate, giving him the kind of boundaries and mothering he'd sure as hell never had. God knew, the boy needed that. In just a week, he'd already begun losing that haunted, hunted look around his eyes, and the hollows of his cheeks were starting to be less pronounced.

And though Malcolm would rather have his thumbs screwed than admit it, he actually kind of liked the softening touches she'd added. They made his flat feel like a home for the first time. Maybe, on some level, he'd been denying himself that luxury all these years as a punishment for having lost Miranda and Robyn. He hadn't realized how much of a difference those efforts would make. And if his own disposition toward the little Latina whirl-wind was shifting, well, damn it, she was hard to resist. He was actually starting to *like* her, beyond wanting to get his mouth and hands back on her.

Malcolm had no idea what to do with that.

Attraction was basic biology. That made sense to him. She was a beautiful woman. But getting to see her in this mothering role was a whole other side he found beyond appealing. Which was ridiculous. He was long past that stage of his life. He'd lost his family and never thought to have another. And yet, here he was, with a teenage boy by his side, waiting patiently for his next instruction, and the knowledge that he'd be seeing a woman on the other side of the dinner table tonight.

Life was pretty fucking strange.

"Hold the end of the tape there. That's a good lad." Malcolm paced over to where the new half-wall was meant to end and called out the measurement.

Gavin scribbled it down in the little notebook he carried. They repeated the process with a handful of other spots and angles before starting over to measure them a second time.

Gavin frowned. "We already did this. Why do it again?"

"People make mistakes. They read the tape wrong or transpose the numbers. There's a saying. 'Measure twice, cut once.'"

"Because if you measure wrong the first time and you cut your lumber, then you're out materials?"

The kid's quick uptake pleased him. "Aye. That's it exactly. Safer to take a few extra minutes to check yourself."

They completed the second round of measurements. As they were headed outside to begin cutting, Gavin's foot knocked into a stack of supplies, sending the loose tiles they'd hauled over from another job site crashing to the floor. Instantly, he cringed, falling to his knees to pick up the pieces, babbling. "I'm sorry. I'm such a clumsy idiot! I'm sorry!"

Malcolm wished he could plant a fist in Simon Elliot's face.

Moving slowly, so as not to spook the lad, he knelt and began helping him gather up the mess. "It's fine. No harm done. These were just leftovers. Don't cut yourself."

For a few long moments, they worked in silence. But Malcolm's conscience wouldn't allow him to stay quiet. "My old man was a right bastard about stuff like that, too. Least while he was paying any attention to me at all. More often than no', he was off his face, shouting at the telly about whatever football match he was losing money on. Which was basically all of them. It was better when he forgot about me."

Gavin cast him a wary look. "What about your ma?"

"Left us both when I was wee. My da liked to blame that on me, too, when the truth was, he was a shite husband. Took me a long time to wrap my head around the idea of that. That his bad behavior wasn't something I had to own." He added another shard to the bucket. "The thing is, just because you've been through something awful, been treated as less than by a person who's supposed to care for you, doesn't mean that's how it's supposed to be. That's a reflection on them, not you." He met the boy's gaze. "Understand?"

Before the boy could reply, someone knocked on the doorjamb.

Malcolm rose, putting himself between Gavin and the new arrival. But it was Raleigh. "I didn't hear you arrive."

"Came on horseback. Icarus needed some exercise. Sorry to interrupt. I wanted to come out and see the latest progress and meet our newest employee." He offered a quick smile to Gavin. "Hey there. I'm Raleigh Beaumont."

Gavin edged closer to Malcolm. "Hullo."

Malcolm didn't blame him for being nervous. He felt a little on pins and needles himself, though Charlotte had said she'd squared everything with Raleigh. The fact was, Raleigh was ultimately the boss, and he had a say in all this.

If the younger man was bothered by the show of anxiety, he didn't show it. He stepped inside and rocked back on booted heels, shoving his hands into the back pockets of his jeans. "I've been looking forward to meeting you. Charlotte's had lots of good things to say."

At the mention of his current favorite person, Gavin came out of his shell a little. "You've talked to Charlotte?"

Raleigh grinned. "Every day. She's basically my second mom. Raised me from the time I was not much older than you."

That got the lad's attention. "Really?"

"Yep. My mama got sick and passed away. Charlotte was her best friend. I don't know where I'd be without her. You're in fantastic hands with her."

"She's really nice."

"The nicest. Hell of a cook, too." He took a step closer and lowered his voice to a conspiratorial tone. "Word to the wise, though. Don't slam doors around her. She's got a thing about that. Last time I forgot, I was on dish duty for more than a week!"

"No' since you were a kid, though, right?"

"Oh, heck no. That was last month."

Malcolm had no idea whether the confession was true, but it dragged a smile out of the kid. He relaxed a little. At least until Raleigh turned to him.

"I just wanted to get the update on things, since we've been missing each other and haven't had our usual estate meetings."

Shoulders going tight, Malcolm started to apologize. "About that—"

Raleigh waved that away. "You've had bigger things to worry about. It's not a problem. Just give me the overview. Is there anything I need to take off your plate so you can finish this?"

Knowing they needed to discuss business, Malcolm turned to Gavin. "Can you take our measurements and start marking the 2x4s?"

Happy to have a task, Gavin brightened. "Aye."

"No touching the saw," Malcolm warned.

"Yes, sir."

"And mind you don't walk up behind the horse."

"Got it!"

They both watched him step outside and head to the trailer of building materials.

Once he was out of earshot, Malcolm eyed his boss. "Are you really okay with this?"

"I trust Charlotte's judgment, and I trust yours. Whatever's needed, Kyla and I are here for it."

Some tension Malcolm hadn't been aware of carrying relaxed a little. Maybe he should've talked to Raleigh sooner. "All right." Shifting gears, he began filling Raleigh in on everything that had come up over the past week regarding the estate.

They'd barely begun when another vehicle pulled up to the cottage.

Malcolm's pulse leapt, and he bolted for the door, automatically looking for Gavin. The lad had paused in his task and was eying the 4x4 that had arrived.

Connor MacKean slid out of the driver's seat and lifted a hand in a wave. "I'm about to be making Charlotte verra verra happy."

"Oh? How's that?" Malcolm asked.

"Oh, well, I found that wrought iron tree thing she wanted for Number Seven. Thought I'd bring it by for her to look at." Connor ducked into the backseat and hauled out the thing.

It was, down to the detail, exactly what she'd described. A literal twisted metal tree, with wee hooks on the branches for mugs.

Something about the whole situation smelled fishy. "You found it?"

Connor rubbed at the back of his neck. His gaze darted to Raleigh. "Aye. I had good luck tracking it down."

"Good luck," Malcolm repeated. He'd known this man from the time he'd been a lad younger than Gavin, as he'd been the one intended to marry Afton. It was clear he was hiding something.

"Oh, yeah," Raleigh jumped in. "So you were able to track down the manufacturer from that catalog she showed you?"

Malcolm eyed the Yank. Was he always this bad at lying?

"Aye. Took some digging, and they only had the one left."

The pair of them were full of shite. But whatever secret they were keeping was their own business. It didn't affect him or

Gavin, so he'd let it lie. "Well, I'm sure Charlotte will be pleased, but she's no' here."

Connor's step hitched. "Where is she?"

How had Malcolm suddenly become the go-to keeper of her schedule? "Away. She's out with Kyla and Sophie, sourcing new furnishings for some of the upcoming cottages."

"So that's where Sophie's gone off to today," he muttered. "I suppose the stores of extras at the castle have rather been decimated at this point."

"Castle?" Gavin asked.

Connor finally turned his attention to the lad, flashing a friendly smile. "Aye. I live in one."

The boy's eyes went wide. "You're having me on!"

"No. I really do. It's six-hundred-years old. On your next day off, you'll have to come by and see it. I'll give you a tour. I'm Connor MacKean, and I'm guessing you're Gavin." He offered his hand for a shake.

After only a moment's hesitation, Gavin took it. "Nice to meet you."

"Connor's my brother-in-law," Raleigh explained. "I'm married to his sister, Kyla. You'll be meeting her at family dinner later this week, if not before."

"Family dinner?" He shot an uncertain glance at Malcolm.

"First I'm hearing of it." They'd agreed to keep Gavin's presence on the down-low.

"Charlotte said y'all would be there. Anyway, Angus needs a headcount, so he knows how much dessert to make."

Gavin's brows drew together. "Who's Angus?"

"Angus is my and Kyla's uncle," Connor explained. "He's practicing to audition for *The Great British Bake-Off*, and we're the beneficiaries of all his bakes. It's a pretty great arrangement, all in all."

"Has he said what he's making?" Raleigh asked.

"Dunno. If anybody has requests, now's the time to make them." Connor eyed Gavin. "What's your favorite?"

"I dinna ken. Nobody's ever asked me."

Malcolm's hands flexed with the need to shake Simon Elliot yet again.

But Gavin didn't seem to be bothered by the question. "If he's taking orders for anything, I think I'd like a Bakewell tart. Someone brought one once for a birthday party at school."

"I expect that can be arranged. I'll pass it along," Connor promised.

And as their company began to scatter, with farewells and promises to see each other at family dinner, Malcolm reflected about how he was being pulled right on out of his hermit lifestyle, whether he liked it or not.

———

"That's my ear!" Gavin's shriek of laughter echoed off the stone barn as he angled his head, only partly trying to get away from a very curious Buttercup, who thought his earlobe was something fun to nibble.

Charlotte grinned. "That's what you get for being down on their level."

He knelt in the grass on hands and knees, cheeks flushed. Bubbles took the opportunity to leap up onto his back for a higher vantage point, baaing her victory over Blossom, who decided to headbutt Gavin in insult. He rolled over to his back, dislodging Bubbles and snagging Buttercup around the middle so she couldn't keep treating his ear as a chew toy. Charlotte quietly took video of him wrestling with the three of them, as only a boy could do.

She wouldn't post it anywhere. This was for her alone. And Malcolm. Proof positive that they were doing the right thing. Less than two weeks in the care of people who truly gave a damn about his welfare, and he was a different boy than the one they'd found hiding out in a derelict cottage. That he still had the capacity for joy after what he'd been through humbled her. Not that he'd said much about his experiences. Just casual comments here and there that intimated significant neglect and abuse. He still flinched and overreacted to anything he deemed a mistake. That was years of conditioning that would take a long time to overcome. If she got her way, they'd have the time to deal with that.

After reading the two of them his version of the riot act for acting outside the system, Hamish had promised to make discreet inquiries to explore their options. So far, he'd been able to confirm that there'd been no missing person's report filed, which wouldn't exactly look good for Simon Elliot in the eyes of social services or a judge when it came down to it. But they were being excruciatingly careful about how they proceeded. She and Malcolm had elected to be vague about what they told Gavin until they had concrete information. The most important thing right now was that no one would be taking him away. She was pretty sure Malcolm would go to war if they tried.

This paternal side of him was unexpected and incredibly appealing. She'd never have imagined the Grumpasaurus Rex she'd been verbally sparring with since early summer to have such a capacity for patience. It made her wonder what he'd been like as a young father to Miranda, before cancer stole her away. These hints of gruff gentleness suggested he'd probably been a good one. His efforts were sometimes awkward, likely because those skills were incredibly rusty after all these years. But he was trying. And much as that had been a shock, Charlotte believed Gavin was bringing a part of Malcolm back to life that he'd allowed to wither and die out of grief. She didn't know why he was allowing it, except that just maybe he was ready to start to live again. She couldn't stop herself from wondering if that would include romantic entanglements as well.

"Are you thinking about Malcolm?"

Charlotte pulled her focus back to Gavin, who peered up at her from the grass, all three lambs tucked in his arms. "Hmm? Why do you ask?"

"Your face went all funny like it does sometimes when you look at him and you don't think anyone else is looking."

Heat crept up her throat, making her grateful for the lowering sun. Was she that obvious? Of course, she had some kind of feelings for Malcolm. They'd embarked on joint parenthood together. And then there was that kiss they *still* hadn't been able to talk about. She was starting to think they never would, and that he'd chalked the whole thing up to a mistake. But she wasn't about to say any of that to her ward.

The sound of approaching vehicles saved her from having to answer.

"That'll be Connor and Angus. And it looks like Sophie's right behind them. Put the triplets back in their pen for the night, and let's head on up to the manor house. You can set the table while I put the finishing touches on dinner."

Gavin's long, measured look told her he hadn't missed her evasion tactic. "Yes, ma'am."

They walked into the best kind of chaos. Connor was setting a dessert case on the counter. Kyla had one arm linked through her uncle's, a gesture as much of affection as worry. Munro, Angus's "friend", who was secretly probably more, looked on with quiet amusement curling his lips. They all kept a much closer eye on Angus since he'd had his heart attack a few months before. At the table, Sophie was unbundling some flowers, and Raleigh was peering into the pot on the stove.

"Raleigh Beaumont, you put that pot lid back before I find my wooden spoon!"

He snapped straight with a comically serious who-me? face and stepped back, both hands raised as proof of his innocence.

She fixed him with her Mom eye. "Let's make introductions, then show Gavin where the utensils are and help him set the table."

"Yes'm," Raleigh nodded.

If any of the group thought Gavin's presence was odd or noted his nerves at meeting them, none of them showed it. They were all friendly and teasing, accepting him into the fold simply because she'd asked. The sight of it had a warm glow setting up in her chest as she went to stir the gravy for the pot roast.

Malcolm arrived as she was getting ready to dish up the food. He shut the door quietly, toeing off his dirty work boots and leaving them in the tray by the door for that purpose. His gaze met hers, a question in a single look.

How's the lad?

She smiled and tipped her head to where Gavin sat in animated discussion with Angus and Munro at the freshly decorated table.

Some tension bled out of his shoulders. He lifted his nose, sniffing. "Something smells good."

"Hope you brought your appetite. I cooked for an army."

His eyes warmed. "I could eat."

The kids helped take all the serving dishes to the table, then everyone sat and began passing plates so they could be filled family-style. Charlotte could barely contain herself from bouncing in her seat. She loved nothing more than having her whole family around one table for a meal, and this motley crew was her unconventional family in Scotland.

"Connor, I've been meaning to thank you for the mug tree. It's exactly what I wanted, and it looks utterly perfect."

His cheeks turned ruddy. "Oh, it was nothin'. Glad I could help."

"What is it he's found?" Sophie asked.

"This utterly exquisite wrought iron tree for mugs," Charlotte explained. "If I'd custom ordered the thing, it couldn't have been more perfect. I was just dreaming, but Connor managed to track one down."

Sophie eyed him from across the table. "Do you have some kind of shopping superpower I've never known about? Because that's a skill your sister and I could use."

Connor's eyes didn't quite meet hers. "Oh, I was just lucky."

Two seats down, Raleigh shook his head, but hid the gesture

by taking another bite of the food. He knew something about why Connor was acting so squirrelly. Was it about the mug tree or about Sophie? Much as Charlotte wanted to know, she decided she had enough on her metaphorical plate and let it go.

Conversation was, as always, fast and furious, with topics bouncing from business to jokes to gossip in the village. As candles burned low, plates and bowls were emptied, and dessert was served. Gavin declared the Bakewell tart Angus had brought the best dessert he'd ever eaten, which had the old man's ears pinking with pleasure. Then the meal was over.

Kyla pushed back from the table. "Sophie and I need to do some work on the final details for a client meeting we've got tomorrow. If anybody needs us, we'll be in my office."

Connor gestured to his uncle. "I'm gonna get this one home, so he has time for his evening cuppa before bed." They all knew Angus tired out pretty quickly these days, though he'd improved considerably since his heart surgery.

"Munro, I've got that book I promised to loan you, if you want to stop by the house on the way home," Angus announced.

"Aye. I can do that."

Raleigh cleared his plate to the counter by the sink. "Gavin, you wanna come with me out to the stable to meet the horses properly?"

Gavin's eyes went wide with excitement as he swung toward Charlotte. "Can I?"

She'd intended for him to do some dishes, but couldn't say no in the face of his pleasure at the notion. "Go on."

After a flurry of movement and farewells, suddenly she was alone with Malcolm for the first time in days.

He placed his own plate on the counter. "Well, it seems we've been left to dish duty." He began to roll up his sleeves, exposing those muscular forearms in a slow reveal she knew wasn't meant to be a tease but was, anyway. "I'll wash. You dry. You know where everything goes."

"Sure."

As he filled the sink with soapy water, she put the minuscule quantity of leftovers in a container and added it to the fridge. The silence between them felt heavy with things unsaid. It wasn't awkward, exactly. More... meaningful. Charlotte wondered if he was thinking of the kiss as she was.

They were alone. Now was her chance to bring it up and clear the air. Even if he wanted to just forget it, she needed to say *something*, just to have resolution for herself.

Eyes focused on the platter she was drying, she took a breath. "I've been wanting to talk to you."

Malcolm spoke over her. "About what happened the night we found Gavin."

They looked at each other and shared a bit of a laugh.

"You go first." Better she see what he had to say before revealing her own thoughts. "What about that night?"

"Well, no' when we found him. The... before. In the kitchen."

Yep, he was definitely talking about the kiss.

"Oh?" Her voice came out half an octave higher than usual.

Her heart sped up as she waited to see where he was going. If he thought it was a mistake, it just might devastate her.

"I havenae been able to stop thinking about it." He sucked in a breath. "And about doing it again."

Relief and heat washed through her in equal measure. Setting the dry platter aside, she looked pointedly around the empty kitchen. "Nobody's stopping you."

On a growl, he reached for her, those big hands curling around her hips and drawing her in. She was with him, rising to her toes so they were hip to hip, chest to chest as their mouths met. Her first thought was that it hadn't been a fluke. Desire flared, chasing through her body like a lit fuse, until it sparked a deeper wanting that had her opening her mouth for him. Her last coherent thought as his tongue touched hers was *More.*

Nothing interrupted them this time. Nothing stopped him from taking the kiss deeper by degrees, devouring her every bit as throughly as he'd devoured her food. The taste of him slid into her, rich and heady and so incredibly potent. Charlotte couldn't remember the last time she'd *wanted* like this and found herself pressing closer, needing more contact, more friction, more everything.

He was vibrating with as much pent-up lust as she was by the time they broke apart.

In another time and another place, maybe they'd have followed through on it. But they were in someone else's kitchen now, and they had more than themselves to consider.

Still, she couldn't stop herself from stroking a finger over the pounding pulse in his throat as she looked up into eyes gone dark with arousal. "What are we going to do about this? Because our lives have gotten pretty complicated and intertwined in the last ten days."

Malcolm didn't flinch. "The smart thing would probably be to focus on Gavin. Keep things simple."

He wasn't wrong, but that definitely wasn't what she wanted to hear.

"But..."

"But?" Her tone was unapologetically full of hope.

He tightened his hold, pulling her closer to the hardness behind his kilt. "I'm no' feeling particularly smart right now."

"Thank God," she breathed, her mind already performing gymnastics to figure out how they could carve out some alone time to finish this.

"I think that I'd like to try this. You and me. Together."

There was something in the way he said it that told her he wasn't just talking about a physical entanglement. "Like... a relationship sort of together?"

"Aye."

Her heart tripped into a giddy gallop at the prospect. She hadn't allowed herself to even think in those terms, because he so clearly hadn't been emotionally available. Maybe he was only dipping a toe back into those waters, but she'd take what she could get.

"I'd like that, too." Cognizant of the fact that this decision impacted their bigger world, she laid down her one rule. "If things don't work out on this front, we can't let it impact Gavin. We're the first stability he's ever known. We can't screw that up."

"Agreed."

They stared at each other in hungry silence.

"Okay," she said, at last. "We're doing this."

"Brilliant." He released her and turned back to the sink.

Ever practical, her Malcolm. *Her* Malcolm. Because at this moment, for now, he was.

Rather than engaging in the schoolgirl squee she was feeling, she returned to her drying duty. Dishes still had to be done.

As she bent over to put the stock pot back in the cabinet, Malcolm shut off the water.

"Did you bring a coat?"

She straightened and brushed the hair back from her face. "No. Why?"

His lips twitched, his eyes sparkling. "Because you have my wet handprint on your arse."

TEN

"What's that supposed to be?"

Malcolm eyed the snarl of bright red yarn in Charlotte's lap and decided Gavin was a braver soul than he for asking.

"Well, if it comes out the way it's supposed to, it will be a sweater." She held up a picture of something that was definitely a jumper, then frowned down at the mess. "I think I've missed a step somewhere."

The misshapen thing looked like the bastard child of Red Riding Hood and Cthulhu. No matter who she intended the thing for, there wasn't a chance in hell it would fit. Not that Malcolm would dare to point that out. Knitting was the third hobby Charlotte had tried out in the past month. The watercolor landscapes had been more Picasso than Monet. The needle felted replicas of the triplets hadn't turned out any better, and her spare bedroom was turning into a graveyard of abandoned supplies.

Gavin considered the lump. "Maybe you should have started with a scarf. Baby steps, aye?"

With a mock scowl, she tossed a ball of yarn at his head with surprisingly good aim, startling a laugh out of the lad when it bounced off his brow. Malcolm didn't think he'd ever tire of that laugh.

Charlotte shoved the lot of it back into the bag she'd brought. "Where can I find a turkey to cook?"

"A turkey?" Malcolm blinked at the non sequitur. "Why?"

"Because Thanksgiving's coming up. I know that's not really a thing over here, but Raleigh and I always celebrate. I make his mama's cornbread dressin' and sweet potato casserole, and at least two kinds of pie, and we talk about everything we're thankful for. It's kind of like a formalized gratitude practice with food, and since I've got a great many things to be thankful for, I figured I'd drag everybody else in, too."

In all seriousness, Gavin raised his hand. "I dinna ken what half of that stuff is, but I volunteer as tribute to eat all of it."

She ruffled his hair. "Always thinking with your stomach."

"It's a wise man who does anything he can to get more of your cooking."

"Flatterer." Beaming, she blew him a kiss, then turned her gaze on Malcolm. "What about you?"

"I agree with the lad about your cooking, so I'll do what I can to help you find a turkey." And they did have a lot to be grateful for.

Over the past few weeks, Hamish had managed discrete inquiries in Duntyre and discovered that Gavin's school had contacted Simon about his son's lack of attendance and been told he'd gone to live with his mother. The mother Hamish had already confirmed formally relinquished her parental rights when she left five years before. Malcolm couldn't imagine doing that to a child. At least he'd had the illusion that his own mum might come back. Either way, they were in a holding pattern, with Hamish working on the best means of handling the situation, while still keeping it out of the system. He'd advised them that the only way that really worked was if Simon signed over his parental rights, which would inevitably lead to some kind of confrontation. Malcolm didn't know how that would go, and he was braced for a fight. Hamish was working on building the case to convince Simon it was in *his* best interest to comply. But for right now, the important thing was that no one was looking for Gavin and the boy was starting to feel safe. That was worth a hell of a lot.

Charlotte cuddled up against him. That was something else Malcolm was thankful for. He'd never in his life imagined himself as a snuggler. Robyn hadn't been this physically affectionate. No one in his life had. But Charlotte expressed affection through touch. Hugs. A hand on the arm. Linking fingers. And Malcolm found that he liked it. The warmth of her was grounding in a way he hadn't expected and definitely hadn't known he'd needed. Maybe some of it was that he was starved for physical touch after his years of solitude. Or maybe it was just her. Either way, it had become their new habit to settle on the sofa together after dinner, while Gavin sprawled in the chair, and they all watched an episode of something or other on TV. It had taken Malcolm a little time to get used to the arrangement, as he still felt weird performing any kind of PDA in front of the lad.

They hadn't hidden the change in their relationship from him, but they'd necessarily been taking things at a snail's pace. Malcolm had to admit—to himself, at least—that was probably a good thing. As much as he wanted Charlotte, he was afraid of screwing it up. It wasn't like he was a good bet. He'd deliberately shuttered his heart years ago and held everyone at arm's length.

The last person he'd allowed himself to care for was Afton. It had been six months since she'd left, and still no word. He hoped she was safe and happy, doing well wherever she'd landed in the world. On some level, he understood that she'd done what she felt she had to, in order to get out of a ridiculous situation. But it still hurt that she hadn't talked to him about it, and hadn't reached out since the pact was resolved. Maybe he'd cared more than she did. Or maybe it was that she hadn't known how much he cared, because he'd let himself become so closed off, only ever showing so much.

As he wrapped his arm tighter around Charlotte and glanced

over at the boy who'd helped drag him back into the land of the living, he vowed that he'd do better with them. *For* them. Even if it took baby steps. The truth was, he was *feeling* for the first time in years, and it was absolutely terrifying. With the two of them, he'd found his way to contentment, and that was a pretty amazing thing. But on the heels of that was always the fear that he'd lose it.

She nestled closer, her hand settling on his knee, fingers tracing lazy patterns there as she watched the screen. It was all too easy to imagine her trailing that hand higher, up the inside of his thigh, to wrap around his cock. His body stirred, and he promptly slammed a mental door on that fantasy, giving her arm a gentle pinch until she glanced up. Her face was set in innocent lines, but her eyes told a different story. Those dark liquid pools were impish and full of banked heat. Malcolm scowled at her, which only made her grin. But she stopped playing with his knee.

As the show wrapped, Malcolm glanced at the clock. "Time to get ready for bed. Early start in the morning. I'm gonna walk Charlotte home." Which he'd been doing every night, simply for the chance to kiss her, since he felt weird doing it in front of the kid.

Gavin rolled out of the chair and smirked. Yeah, he knew. And clearly, he thought the pair of them were the funniest thing ever.

Whatever. Malcolm wasn't quite ready to break out of the headspace of taking things slowly in front of him.

Charlotte rose and pulled him in for a hug and a smacking kiss on the cheek. "Good night, sweet boy. I'll see you tomorrow."

"Night, Charlotte." With a salute and another smirk, he headed upstairs.

She gathered her knitting bag, and Malcolm walked her next door. As they stepped inside, she turned to him. "We're not fooling him."

He shut the door and backed her against it. "I'm not trying to. Call me old-fashioned, but I definitely dinna want to do any of the things I'd like to do to you in front of him."

On that note, he took her mouth as he'd wanted all day,

drinking in that little gasp of pleasure as she rose to him, wrapping her arms around his shoulders. The erection he'd managed to will away sprang instantly to life, demanding attention. Charlotte hummed, pressing closer, making his vision go white behind his eyes for a few moments as she rubbed against him. Malcolm struggled to rein it in, to find some control.

She nipped at his bottom lip. "Malcolm, I appreciate your desire not to emotionally scar the child, but it's just a little mean of you to keep riling me up like this and walking away, leaving me to relieve my own suffering."

Well, fuck. Now he was thinking about her pleasuring herself while thinking of him. That didn't do a damned thing to help the situation.

"I want to take my time with you," he growled. "Because that's what you deserve."

Her fingers dove into his hair, tugging a little as she urged him to look at her. "I appreciate that, and I sure as hell look forward to it, but please, for the love of God, help me take the edge off. You have no idea how long it's been."

He'd never claimed to be a noble man, and he wanted to see her eyes go blind with passion, wanted to see that beautiful face flush as she came apart.

"Well, since you asked so nicely." His hands gripped her hips, lifting her up until she could wrap her legs around his waist. Then he pressed her against the door again, his cock nestled between her legs.

Charlotte sighed. "Oh, yes. Please."

He trailed his lips along the column of her throat. "I like it when you say please."

"I like everything about what you're doing."

She felt fucking fantastic, writhing against him, and he tried not to think about how easy it would be to strip off her jeans, flip up his kilt, and slide into her. He was not going to take her against a door their first time. But he was confident he could leave her satisfied before he walked out, and give himself more fodder for the shower later.

Surging against her, he slipped his hands beneath her sweater, up her torso to cup her magnificent breasts. They were full and heavy in his hands, the nipples pulled to taut nubs he desperately wanted to taste. But she was busy devouring his mouth, rocking against him with a breathy little whimper that told him she was already close. He rolled her nipples, loving the moan it wrenched from her, and how she seemed to be trying to press against him everywhere at once. She was one big bundle of arousal, and that was basically the hottest thing ever. He swiveled his hips harder against her center, thrusting his tongue into her mouth, following the rhythm of her rocking until she locked her legs around him and groaned long and low into his mouth.

With vicious satisfaction, Malcolm held her through her shuddering release and after, until she laid her head limply on his shoulder.

"Well, I'd say that qualifies as dulling the edge."

"Good." He kissed her again, gently this time, and let her slide down his body.

She eyed the erection tenting the front of his kilt. "Seems I ought to do the same."

But before she could get her hands on him, he twisted his hips away. "No. That was for you. I'll take care of that in the shower."

Charlotte's lips, full and rosy from his, rolled out in a pout. "You're taking the shower over me?"

"If you get your hands on me, I won't be walking out this door, and I sure as fuck won't be quiet about it. We may not be fooling Gavin about anything, but that's a line I dinna want to cross while he's within earshot."

As fresh heat flared in her eyes, she dropped her hands. "Fair enough. But just so you know, I'm going to need more than that preview in the very near future."

Gripping her by the nape, he hauled her in for one more fierce kiss. "Noted. Good night, Charlotte."

"Good night."

And with one last glance at her satisfied glow, he stepped outside and shut the door.

————

Charlotte's head was not on the task at hand, which was a problem, considering that task was painting the walls of the next cottage. They were already behind schedule, so the last thing they needed was some kind of accident with the paint damaging the floors or splashing onto the cabinets. But how could she think about decorating after the phone call she'd had from Hamish right before coming out here? Especially with the subject of that phone call quietly dipping a roller into a paint tray and smoothly spreading a pale fawn shade onto the wall across the room. A fight was coming, and soon.

She wished Malcolm was here to discuss this with. But he was off handling estate business with some tenants, so she was left with the frantic hamster wheel of her own thoughts and a far-too-perceptive teenage boy she wanted to protect at all costs.

"Earth to Charlotte."

"Hmm?" Gavin was staring at her in a way that suggested this wasn't the first time he'd called her name. "I'm sorry, baby. My head's somewhere else today."

"You're worried." He didn't pose it as a question.

"What makes you say that?"

"You've got that scrunch between your eyebrows."

A poker player, she was not.

"It's about me, isn't it?" Absently, he reloaded the roller. "I know I can't just stay with you like this forever."

This kid.

She and Malcolm hadn't talked too much about the future with Gavin because they hadn't wanted to worry him until there was something concrete to share. But it was obvious the boy *was* worried, and she wanted to be honest with him. The truth likely wasn't as terrifying as whatever he'd make up in his head while waiting for her to talk things over with Malcolm first.

She held out a hand. "Come sit with me."

Pleased when he took it without hesitation, she flipped over a couple of 5-gallon buckets and gestured to their makeshift seats. Knowing the importance of getting this right, she faced him, knee to knee, keeping his hand in hers as she openly met his gaze.

"So, you know we contacted our attorney friend, Hamish Colquhoun, about what we needed to do so you'll be protected."

Gavin nodded, his eyes already shuttering in preparation for the worst-case scenario.

After the openness they'd fostered this past month, seeing that regression, that automatic expectation of disappointment, absolutely broke her heart.

"That was essential from the front end, whether you decided you wanted to stay or not. We wanted to make sure no one would make you go back to your father. Part of that has involved Hamish gathering character witnesses against him. Proof that he's not been good to you or for you. That's taken some time, because he's trying to be as discrete as possible to avoid tipping off anybody to where you are. Not only your dad, but also social services. We're doing everything in our power to avoid involving the authorities because, once we do, we lose control of the situation."

"They'll take me away." It wasn't a question. The grim set of his jaw told her he understood the gravity of the situation.

Charlotte nodded. "Neither Malcolm nor I are certified foster parents, so they couldn't legally leave you with us. And there are some other potentially thorny issues for me because I'm not a citizen of the UK. I'm only here on a work visa. That's something that could change eventually, but, again, it takes time. So far, none of that is a problem, and we hope it'll stay that way."

"But?"

Of course, the kid would recognize the 'but' she wasn't saying.

Charlotte tightened her hold on his hand. "Malcolm and I

have wanted you to stay from the beginning. We like having you around. You're good company, a good worker, and you've become a valuable member of our weird little unconventional family. Before we get into the rest of this, I need to ask you an important question."

Wariness crept into his expression. "Okay."

"Do you want to stay with us? He and I feel like things have gone really well the past month. But none of that matters if you'd rather go somewhere else. And it's your choice. We'll fight as hard as we can to make sure that it's your choice." She hoped like hell circumstances didn't turn her into a liar.

"I dinna want to leave."

A tension around her heart loosened a little. "Even though you're totally going to have to start school in January if you stay?"

A flicker of amusement twitched his lips. "Aye, even so. I like it here. I like the triplets and Mabel and the other animals. And I like you and Malcolm."

Blinking back the gathering tears, Charlotte kept her tone matter-of-fact. "Okay. Then we'll do whatever we have to so you can stay. At the end of the day, your father has to give up his rights to you as a parent—either because a court takes them away after determining he's unfit, or by signing them directly away to someone else, who can apply as your legal guardian or guardians. The second route is the easiest, and that's what we're hoping for."

"Easy?" Gavin stared at her. "You think he's going to make it easy? He'll be like a dog wi' a bone. He disnae care about me, but he disnae want anyone else to either. He willnae agree to that."

"Not if we just walked up to him and asked, no. But we're smarter than that. All those character witnesses Hamish is getting statements from... he's not just pulling those together to give to social services. He's essentially building a case for your father. To pressure him into believing that he's going to get into serious trouble for everything he's done to you when we turn all that information over to the authorities—unless he gives permission for guardianship to us."

And that was the crux of what agitated that hamster in her brain—because becoming legal guardians of Gavin would constitute a serious commitment. A life-changing commitment. Not only to him, but between her and Malcolm. Certainly, things between them had been going well. But in a huge sense, the past month had been a honeymoon period for their strange little found family. If things went off the rails for their relationship, would they be able to successfully co-parent in a way that wasn't damaging to Gavin?

"And if he doesn't?"

"Honestly, I don't know. No doubt the authorities would get involved. Malcolm and I can certainly take whatever steps would be necessary to get whatever certifications we needed to keep you legally, and we've got a lot of people willing to be character references for us on the good side."

"But you said there was that thing about you only being here on a work visa. What if they won't let you because of that?"

"That's more stuff I don't know yet."

"What if you had something that overrode a work visa?"

"I don't know what that would be."

"You and Malcolm could get married."

Charlotte nearly choked on her own spit. Yes, she cared for Malcolm. She was sure as hell attracted to him. She was enjoying this dance they were doing, working their way toward something more serious. And certainly, she trusted him enough that they'd essentially adopted a child together. But *marriage?*

"That's kind of getting ahead of things, kiddo."

"Is it? You like each other. More than like each other."

"We do, but—"

"Is it me? Because I'm a cock blocker?"

She felt light-headed as all the blood drained out of her face, then rushed back in furious embarrassment. "First off, let's not use that term, okay? Second, things between Malcolm and me are complicated. We're taking our time exploring this new dynamic." And if they were taking more time than she really wanted because of their little teenage chaperone, that definitely wasn't something she was admitting to said chaperone out loud.

"Well, it's no' like you can easily date while you're both babysitting me."

"Dating isn't our first priority, right now. You are."

"Which I appreciate. But you deserve some alone time for… whatever."

Charlotte absolutely could not cope with the idea of this kid thinking about her and Malcolm whatevering.

"Anyway, Raleigh invited me over for the night for a *Star Wars* movie marathon. He says I haven't been properly educated until I've seen the original trilogy. We'll be staying in, so I'm safe, and you and Malcolm can go out. Like on a date."

Her already overworked brain ground to a halt. "Wait, have you talked to Raleigh about me and Malcolm?"

The boy blinked at her. "Was I not supposed to?"

They hadn't announced the change of their relationship to anyone else. They hadn't talked about it or defined it other than between each other. She couldn't quite decide how she felt about the man who was basically her son knowing she was involved with anyone. Let alone his estate manager. It wasn't as if she were embarrassed, but the whole thing was so very new, and had been complicated almost from the beginning by the presence of Gavin.

Woman up, cupcake.

"No, baby, it's fine. It's just a little awkward because I haven't dated anybody in a really long time."

"Well, now I'm taken care of for the night, so you can start."

"Well, okay then."

ELEVEN

Shower and a shave: Check.

Black button-down shirt pressed: Check.

Boots cleaned and polished: Check.

Mortification that his ward had made arrangements to take himself off for the night to give them some alone time for a date night—along with suggestions on what that date should entail: Check.

The lad was certain Malcolm had no game. And, okay, he'd been out of it long enough that whatever skills he possessed were rusty. But he still had a notion of how to woo a woman. More importantly, he had a clear understanding of his own limitations and knew when to call in reinforcements. That request had been its own form of awkward, but his coconspirators assured him everything would be sorted, despite the short notice.

The only thing remaining was to pick up his date.

A knock on his door had him scowling. If anyone needed a bloody thing and ran this night off the rails, Malcolm just might kill them.

But it wasn't a tenant or Raleigh or any of their handful of other employees standing on his stoop. It was Charlotte herself.

She was gorgeous, dressed in some kind of dark red wrap dress that hugged every one of her curves. She'd paired it with knee-high leather boots and a smart little leather jacket. The only thing stopping his tongue from falling right out of his mouth in a drool was the look on her face. It wasn't panic, exactly, but it definitely wasn't excitement either.

"What's wrong?"

"Raleigh just stopped by to pick up Gavin."

And saw her looking like this? No question she was ready for a date. "So... he knows about us?"

She scooped the hair back from her face with a nod.

"Did he hassle you?"

"No. He told me to enjoy myself." The pinch on her face suggested she definitely wasn't.

Shite. Maybe this had been a bad idea. Maybe faced with actually *telling* people about them, she'd realized she didn't want this. Didn't want him.

"And that's a... problem?"

"No, I just... feel strange about the whole thing."

Malcolm considered tiptoeing around the issue and decided that would just waste precious time. Better to rip the bandage off. "About us? Or about the fact that Raleigh now knows?"

"I feel fine about us. It's just... we—you and I—feel like a very personal thing. I've dated over the years since I took over Raleigh's care, but it was always something I kept very separate from him. And I just don't know how to feel about the fact that apparently he and Gavin are playing matchmaker."

Malcolm wasn't entirely sure how he felt about it either, but he wasn't going to fight it, as their interference was getting him exactly what he wanted. God and Charlotte willing. "Do you want to call the whole thing off?"

"What? No!" She stepped inside, laid a hand on his chest. "No, I'm just still processing having different sectors of my life collide. I definitely still want this."

The night? Or him? Both?

Only one way to find out.

He snagged the keys to his 4x4. "Then let's go."

When this relatively last-minute opportunity had presented itself, he'd made the executive decision against taking her out to The Stag's Head. Showing up in the local pub wouldn't give them the kind of privacy they'd both been craving, not with everybody and their brother stopping by to say hello, as was the way of small villages. He'd elected not to drive to one of the other nearby villages, either. Not when they had ready access to options that had already been kitted out to be comfortable and inviting.

When he pulled up in front of the cottage, Charlotte frowned. "What are we doing here? Is there something wrong we need to handle for guests before we go to dinner?"

"No. Nothing's wrong. I just thought we'd both be more comfortable having our date away from prying eyes, so I booked it for the evening." He also *really* hoped this would lead to some conclusions they'd been denied up to this point.

"Oh. That was thoughtful of you. Thank you."

For once, she waited until he came around to open the passenger door, allowing him to escort her to the cottage. He had no idea what to expect, given the time constraints, but he'd been promised food and ambiance. Turning the key in the lock, he opened the door, and they stepped inside.

A fire crackled in the stone hearth. Flowers were scattered everywhere—in vases and pitchers, draped across the mantle. Petals had been sprinkled over the crisp linens of the freshly made bed in the corner. Electric candles flickered on almost every table or shelf. The whole ambiance had Sophie stamped all over it. A massive basket sat on the rough wood island. He could see the neck of a wine bottle sticking out among an assortment of other goodies nestled inside.

Yet another peculiar look flickered over Charlotte's face. Damn it, Malcolm wished he could read her better.

"What?"

"Did you arrange for all of this?"

"Sort of. I asked Kyla about renting the place for the evening, and she said she'd take care of it. Obviously, she got help from Sophie, with all the flowers. What's wrong?"

She pressed her red-painted lips together for a moment before flashing a sheepish smile. "Nothing's wrong. It's just that they gave us the honeymoon package."

"Ah."

What more could he say? He'd been hoping to romance her. All these trappings were in service to that. But now he understood her discomfort with the idea of others knowing about them. The idea that Kyla and Sophie had set up the cottage with the idea of seduction in mind made him feel a little weird, too. He'd known them as wee girls.

"I just think it's interesting that this is happening right on the heels of Gavin announcing he thinks we should get married."

Malcolm dropped the keys. "He thinks what now?"

"He thinks it would give us a better case for being his custodial guardians if things go awry with Simon. I mean, he's probably not wrong, but... that's a lot."

It sure as hell was. But instead of allowing himself to fall down that rabbit hole, he focused in on the more immediate part of what she'd said. "You talked about Simon with Gavin?"

"In broad strokes. He's a smart boy, and he's worried, so I explained the plan."

It wasn't what they'd agreed to, but he trusted her judgment in this. She'd done a hell of a good job raising Raleigh, so he knew she had good parenting instincts.

"How did he take that?"

"Well, he wants to stay with us."

Some thrumming tension he'd been carrying around for weeks began to relax. "Good." Malcolm didn't think he could take having someone else he cared about walk away.

"I think he's kind of dubious about the likelihood of success of Plan A, so he's worried about the rest. Hence his matchmaking efforts tonight."

It was obvious in the way her fingers nervously plucked at the sleeve of her coat that she was worried about the whole thing. "Do you want to talk through all of it?" That wasn't remotely what he wanted for tonight, but she'd hardly settle in for pleasure if she was stewing in anxiety. And if there were decisions to be made regarding Gavin's welfare, better they face them head on.

Charlotte angled her head in consideration. "Right now, no. Because there's nothing we can do to change the situation tonight, and a lot of people have gone to the trouble to see that we get the night to ourselves. It seems a damn shame to spend that talking about the things we'd be talking about on any given day, anyway. I really just want to spend some time with you."

Reassured, Malcolm grunted and strode over to the island to investigate the contents of the basket. He pulled out the bottle of wine and a pair of glasses. There was also a container of chocolate-covered strawberries that were no doubt Angus's doing, a box of crackers, and a loaf of crusty bread. On the counter, a small slow cooker held what appeared to be some sort of stew. The scent of it already had his stomach growling as he opened the fridge to find a charcuterie board. "Do you want to eat? It looks like they've set us up with all kinds of stuff."

"Malcolm."

He turned around to find her draping her coat around the back of a kitchen chair, her attention wholly on him.

"Eating is not what I have in mind right now."

Oh, thank God. Oh, hell yes.

"It'll keep." He shut the refrigerator and stalked toward her. "What do you want?" Based on the simmering lust in her eyes, he was pretty sure they were entirely on the same page, but confirmation was always smart.

She flowed into him, snaking her arms up his chest to toy with the hair at his nape. "Take me to bed."

Her husky order had his erection reporting for immediate duty. They'd been circling around this for a month. Longer, really, if he considered all that sniping they'd done as some kind of foreplay. It would be so easy to tumble her onto the bed and head straight for sweet relief. But that wasn't what he'd promised. He'd said he wanted to take his time. Given he had no idea when they'd get another opportunity for this, he was sticking to that plan.

Curling his hands around her hips, he pulled her forward, lowering his head for a long inhale as he skimmed his lips along the column of her throat. The scent she'd dabbed there was something spicy and floral that made him think of tropical beaches where swimsuits were optional. "You smell delicious."

"Mmm, you feel delicious." Her hands were bold as they slid up his chest, tracing, molding to the muscles there, even as she tipped her head to one side in blatant invitation.

Accepting that gift, he explored the new angle of her throat and began to slowly back her toward the bed, enjoying the friction of their bodies brushing, separated by only a few layers of fabric. Her fingers worked at his shirt buttons, until she could spread the fabric wide and press her mouth to one pec, tongue darting out to tease his nipple.

"Careful, woman. Turnabout is fair play."

"I'd be very disappointed if it weren't." With one hand, she guided his to the knot tied at her waist.

Malcolm watched her eyes go impossibly darker as his fingers pulled the knot loose. He unwrapped her, parting the sides of the dress until it slipped from her shoulders, leaving her standing there in a confection of black lace that served her breasts up like a feast.

"Fuck me," he murmured, tracing the edge of one bra cup in reverence.

"That is absolutely the idea. Touch me, Malcolm. Taste me. Take me. I want you."

Christ, the woman was going to bring him to the edge with her words alone.

Unwilling to end this so quickly, he dug deep for some control and nudged her to sit on the bed. She leaned back on her elbows, staring up at him with some combination of lust and a dare in her eyes. With slow deliberation, he unzipped the boots.

Charlotte watched him, unmoving, as he slid first one and then the other from her tiny feet. Taking advantage of her position, he reached around to release the catch of her bra, growling in satisfaction as it opened. She slipped it off and reclined back on her elbows again, full, beautiful breasts on display, just for him. But he needed more. He wanted her entirely bare. Hooking his fingers in the waistband of the tiny excuse for a thong she wore, he worked them down her legs, until she wore nothing but a Mona Lisa smile.

"God, I just want to look at you."

"I hope you'll do more than look." She skimmed her own hand down her belly, fingers delving into the thatch of curls at the apex of her thighs. "I'd rather wait for you, but patience isn't really one of my virtues." Her other hand cupped a breast, rolling the nipple between her fingers.

This woman was going to be the death of him.

Scooping her up, he tossed her further back on the bed. The mattress dipped as he crawled up to join her, replacing that hand with his mouth on her breast, and slipping his own fingers beneath hers to explore her slick folds. And, oh, it was even better than he'd imagined hearing her hum of pleasure as he worshipped her. Each time he felt her getting close, he backed off, changing tactics until he felt that gathering again. He licked and sucked and stroked her, until hums turned to moans, and moans turned to incoherent pleas in a torrent of Spanish. When the whip of release flashed through her, strangling his fingers, she was every bit as lovely and flushed as he'd dreamed. And so very wet.

Malcolm slipped his fingers from her core, drinking in her gasps from the aftershocks as she slowly came down from the climax. His cock was straining, demanding some action, but he thought he'd rather torture her with his mouth next, see if he couldn't get her screaming his name.

Charlotte's eyes opened and fixed on his. She struggled up, hands shoving at his shoulders.

Worried, for a moment, that he'd done something wrong, that this was her saying no, he fell back. Releasing her.

"Oh no. I know that look. You can drive me out of my mind later." With more dexterity than he'd expected, she unfastened his kilt, exposing him to her hungry gaze. "And I can assure you, I'll return the favor." She bent, pressing a kiss to the bobbing tip of his erection. "But right now, I need you."

He could've fought her. He was twice her size. But why the hell would he, when the idea of Charlotte Vasquez taking what she wanted was so damned arousing? So was the picture she made, throwing one leg over his hips and rising over him, those magnificent breasts swaying as she lined up his cock with her entrance. Eyes on his, she sank down, taking him in on one long, slow slide.

At the tight wet heat of her, he nearly blacked out, because she was the best fucking thing he'd ever experienced. And as she began to ride him, her breasts swaying, she looked like some kind of pagan goddess. Malcolm thought he'd happily sacrifice himself on this altar for the rest of time. Her body gripped his like a glove, taking him deeper with every undulation. And no matter his good intentions, he knew he wasn't going to last much longer. Clinging to his last vestiges of control, he reached between them, thumbing her clit until she detonated, dragging him with her into the fire.

Later—a long time later—Malcolm returned to consciousness. Surrounded by flowers and candles and the scents of good food and sex, with a warm, naked woman draped over his chest, her leg threaded with his, he felt complete and utter contentment.

Rousing himself enough to stroke her hair, he pressed a kiss to her temple. "You know, I have a new appreciation for all the posh little touches you insisted we have at these places. It really does add to the ambiance."

Charlotte began to laugh, a little giggle at first that morphed into great gasping hilarity. She was still laughing when he kissed her and rolled her beneath him.

———

Charlotte was sore in places she hadn't known she could still get sore. And that was saying something, since she'd been doing home renovations for the past several months. But oh dear Lord, was there anything better than multiple orgasms with an attractive, interesting man who thought you were gorgeous? No, there definitely was not. They were so far and above the self-assisted variety as to not even be on the same scale. Who knew that Malcolm Niall had that much passion pent up behind his stoic mask? As far as she was aware, only her. The knowledge of that felt like some glorious, sexy secret just between the two of them, and she couldn't stop smiling, even as she stood just outside a cottage with multiple broken windows, a chunk of missing roof, and clear evidence a family of rodents had taken up residence.

"Grab the shovel, my boy. We've got work to do."

Picking up the handles of the wheelbarrow, she pushed it inside the next project on her renovation list. She and Gavin would clear out as much as they could, then see what Malcolm wanted to do when he arrived later. He'd been tied up with managerial duties this morning, helping move a flock of sheep from one part of the estate to another. The idea of seeing him again after last night only had the smile spreading wider.

"You're in an exceptionally good mood today," Gavin observed.

"It's a beautiful day that I get to spend with one of my favorite people." Swinging an arm around his shoulders—and holy shit, he'd grown already—she stretched up to press a smacking kiss to his cheek.

"Uh-huh." He passed over a shovel. "Are you sure it disnae have anything to do wi' a usually snarly estate manager? One who was actually whistling before coffee this morning?"

It tickled her to no end that even Malcolm's eternal grumpitude had been obliterated by last night. Schooling her girlish delight into the semblance of a stern expression, she fixed Gavin with a look. "Okay, fine, it *might* have something to do with him.

We appreciate your little matchmaking efforts. But Malcolm and I can take it from here, thank you very much."

"Can you, though? Because Raleigh thinks you'll get in your own way."

Fists balled on her hips, she glared at him. "You're talking about us with Raleigh?"

"Duh." Gavin shrugged shoulders that were far less thin than they'd been a month ago. "I wanted to know if you'd dated anyone before, while you were raising him. He said no."

For a moment, she didn't know what to say. "There were a few people. No one who really mattered, which is why he never knew about them."

"He figured you kinda skipped all that because of him." Gavin scuffed the toe of his shoe against the floor. "I just... I don't want you to do that because of me. You deserve to be happy."

Charlotte's throat went thick with emotion. *This kid.* She pulled him in for a hug. "Thank you, baby. I appreciate that. And we are happy. With each other and with you."

The sound of a footstep had her turning, heart lifting as she expected to see Malcolm in the doorway. She wanted to share this moment with him, as they'd shared countless others. But the hulking shape in the door wasn't Malcolm. He wasn't wearing a kilt, and he moved wrong. But it was the instant snap of tension in Gavin that told her who he was, even before he spoke.

"How touching." The man angled his head, studying her. "So you're Mac's latest whore. I have to say, his taste has improved."

"Don't you talk about her like that!" Gavin shouted.

Simon—because this had to be Simon Elliot—took a lunging step inside. "Don't you take that tone with me, lad." His tone dripped with venom and the kind of mean that was bred into the bone.

The change in Gavin was instant, his terror a palpable thing.

Like Malcolm, Simon was a big man, well over six feet and broad with muscle. But where Malcolm made her feel safe, this man felt like a threat. Charlotte could smell the alcohol on him, though he didn't appear to be staggering drunk. She suspected he was the level of intoxicated that was just enough to exponentially raise the stupid quotient, without dulling the reflexes much. It was a recipe for violence.

In that moment, she was excruciatingly aware they were alone.

Without taking her eyes off Simon, she reached for one of the shovels. "Gavin, get behind me."

His father sneered. "Hiding behind a woman?"

Choking up on her grip, she held the shovel like a baseball bat. "A woman who's going to kick your ass unless you leave this property immediately."

"Sure. I'll leave. But no' without my son."

Fury lit a fire in her blood because she could feel Gavin's vibrating anxiety. "Over my dead body. He's not going anywhere with you."

With an ugly smile, Simon stepped closer.

Fear crawled through her belly. She'd do whatever she could to stop this man, up to and including bodily harm. But what if she wasn't fast enough? The shovel had decent heft, but it was awkward, and she wasn't accustomed to striking a moving target. In her peripheral vision, she assessed the space for other potential weapons. But there was nothing. They hadn't brought in any other tools. Hadn't even gotten started yet on the work. Where the hell was her phone? If she could manage to dial Malcolm... But she had no idea where he was on the estate and whether he even had coverage.

She needed to buy time. Get him talking. If he was talking, he wasn't acting. That gave more opportunity for somebody to drop by. She prayed with everything she had that Raleigh or Connor or one of the others would feel a sudden urge to check on the status of things. There'd be safety in numbers.

"How did you find us here?"

"Somebody was asking questions about me. About my boy. A buddy of mine overheard. Didnae take too much detective work to trace it back to Hamish Colquhoun. Everybody 'round here knows he's thick as thieves with the MacKeans. After that, it just took some well-placed questions at the pub to find out about the boy that got hired on at Lochmara. Didnae expect to find him working with my old mate Mac Niall. Kinda thought he'd have offed himself by now."

The casual way he suggested that Malcolm would've committed suicide had Charlotte's blood turning to ice.

"Come to find out he's running this place. He's come up in the world from the old days. But I ken the truth. No matter what he's done since, Mac's still a drunk. He's still that guy who got so jaked he permanently crippled a bloke in a pub brawl."

She didn't believe him. Malcolm had admitted to turning to the bottle after Miranda died and he lost Robyn. But she didn't for a moment believe that he'd have lost control that badly.

"You know nothing about Malcolm."

Her defense seemed to amuse him. "I know he's taken something that disnae belong to him. I want it back." His gaze slid behind her. "Time to come home, son."

"No." Charlotte tightened her hold on the shovel.

"Do you really think you're going to stop me? A wee slip of a thing like you?" His gaze raked over her, oily and viscous. "Although, with those tits, maybe no' such a slip. A good handful, those."

"You're a cretin."

He made a little lunging motion toward her, pulling back at the last second before she swung. With a twisted grin, he did it again and again. She realized he wasn't going to actively attack her. At least, not without getting her to take a swing first so he could claim self-defense. She just had to hold out until someone could get here.

Oh, please, God. Send someone—anyone—to help.

Simon continued to provoke her, springing and stomping and waving his hands. Charlotte continued to pivot, keeping herself between him and Gavin. Maybe if she could get him to move enough, they could get to the door...

Evidently tiring of the game, Simon darted closer, hands outstretched. She swung, feeling the *whump* of the shovel connecting. But Simon didn't slow. With no effort at all, he twisted, yanking the shovel from her grip. Her tiny hands were no match for his brute strength.

Instinctively, she raised her fists, bracing herself to leap, scratching and pummeling whatever she could reach.

But someone else hurtled through the door with a roar. Simon turned, only to be driven back as Malcolm used momentum to slam him into a wall.

His face twisted with rage, he pressed one forearm across Simon's throat. "Get the fuck away from my family!"

Simon began to laugh. At least, that's what Charlotte thought that noise was, sawing out of his constricted throat.

"Your family? They're no' your family. And I'm no' going to hand over my child just because you were careless enough to lose yours."

For one instant, Malcolm's face went bone white. Then the rage was in control. He drove a fist into Simon's stomach, doubling him over. Simon shoved away from the wall, sending Malcolm staggering back with an uppercut that made his teeth click. With a shake of his head, he was in it again, dealing brutal blows that snapped Simon's head back. Something crunched. Blood sprayed from Simon's face. With a bellow, he retaliated, getting in a couple of jabs before the tide turned yet again.

Someone had to put a stop to this before either of them did more damage. She needed to find her phone. To call for reinforcements. But she couldn't leave Gavin alone in here.

Rushing to where he'd crouched in a corner, tears streaming down his cheeks, she grabbed his hand. "Come on. We have to go."

He let her pull him to his feet, and they skirted the brawling men to get out the door. Charlotte immediately sprinted for the truck. Her phone was, blessedly, still in the cupholder. She dove for it, hesitating for a moment with her thumb over the pad.

Should she call Raleigh? Connor? Or should she go straight for the police? Once they got involved, whatever control she had over the situation was lost.

But as she heard the continued thud of fists on flesh, she understood that control was already gone.

She dialed.

"999. What is your emergency?"

TWELVE

Simon had been arrested. Hauled away in the back of a police car, with blood still streaming from the nose Malcolm had broken. The only reason Malcolm had escaped arrest himself was because of Charlotte and Gavin's testimony that Simon had been threatening them, trying to force Gavin to go with him. The police now knew Gavin was Simon's son. That he'd run away from abuse. That he'd been living at Lochmara. The full details weren't out yet, but an inquiry would happen, and everything they'd worked for this past month would fall apart.

All because Malcolm had failed.

Christ, he couldn't get the image of Charlotte's face out of his mind. That flash of terror and bafflement as Simon wrenched the shovel out of her hands. The resolute way she'd planted her feet and lifted her tiny fists against a monster twice her size.

It curdled his stomach because his brain was more than happy to supply a million and one ways about how she could have been hurt. How Gavin could have been taken. All the things that could have happened to either of the people he loved because he hadn't been there to stop it. There was no joy in the realization that he loved them. Only fear. Fear for what might have happened. Fear for what still could. Because he wasn't enough. He'd never be enough.

His head hadn't stopped ringing yet from the pounding he'd taken at Simon's hands. It didn't matter that he'd given better than he got. He'd snapped, letting himself be further provoked and exposing his family to the rage that always lurked beneath the surface. Exposing that traumatized child to his true capacity for violence. Something he'd vowed never to do.

The soft sound of a footstep on the stairs had him looking up.

"He's finally asleep." Shadows bruised the skin beneath Charlotte's eyes, and her hair was pulled back into a messy tail. Her shoulders dipped with exhaustion, and for once vibrance didn't cast a youthful glow over her familiar features.

The police had allowed them to bring Gavin home after they'd all been released from questioning. Resources were spread thin, and he was safe with them, so nobody had felt there was a need to drag out a social worker just yet. But it was only a matter of time. How much longer would the lad be able to call this home? Did he even still want to, after today?

Charlotte padded across to where Malcolm sat in the living room, automatically reaching to wrap her arms around him. He wanted that hug more than anything in the world. Wanted to burrow into her softness and accept the comfort she offered as easily as breathing. But he didn't deserve such kindness, and it was long past time he stopped taking it. He gently pushed her away.

Worry flickered in her eyes. "I expect the bruises are making themselves known now. Let me clean you up."

She thought it was pain from his injuries. For a moment, he opened his mouth to correct her, then closed it again. He understood her need to do something, and certainly his wounds could use more tending. He'd done only the bare minimum, washing the cuts on his hands and his face at the police station.

She retrieved the first aid kit from the cabinet in the kitchen and opened it, pulling out antiseptic and gauze pads. The sting of it as she dabbed at the cut along his cheek and above his eye was welcome. It kept his brain anchored in the moment instead of the future or the past.

"I'm sorry." His apology came out full of gravel.

Her eyes flicked to his, full of so much kindness. "None of this was your fault."

"I should have been there. I shouldnae have left either of you alone."

"We had no reason to think he'd show up. No reason to believe he had any way of finding us. We were careful."

"How the hell did he even find Gavin?"

"Hamish had his guy asking questions. You know small towns. Somebody overheard something and told him. He followed the breadcrumb trail. Said he heard about the boy hired on out here at the pub."

Malcolm swore.

"Not your fault," Charlotte repeated. "Short of keeping him locked in the house, there was no way to keep the tenants from finding out about him, and without bringing a lot more people in on the secret, we couldn't very well ask them to keep their mouths shut. There was always risk in Hamish asking questions. A confrontation with Simon was already coming. We knew that."

"No' like this. It was meant to be on our terms."

She sat, lifting his hand to clean the splits on his knuckles. "I'm not sure our terms were ever going to work. I think we were naïve."

Seeing the deep concern, his own disquiet ratcheted up a few notches. "Did something else happen before I got there?"

With a shake of her head, she continued to dab on antiseptic. "Not really. He was just talking out his ass. Insulting me. Insulting Gavin. Making bullshit claims about you. That you were a drunk. That you'd crippled someone in a bar fight."

Malcolm flinched as her words hit home. He could tell she didn't believe it.

God, he'd tried to forget. Tried to overcome his past. To be a better man. But he'd never been able to hide from his own shame.

And in this moment, he knew he couldn't hide it from her either. Because he wasn't good enough. Not for her. Not for that child. They both deserved better.

"I did."

Her hands froze on his, and she didn't lift her gaze.

"I was a drunk, exactly as he said. It was the worst time of my life. After losing Miranda and Robyn, I fell into the bottle and didnae come out again for a long, long time. Simon and I were drinking buddies. That's how I knew him, how I knew in an instant what kind of home Gavin was coming from. I was reckless back then. Had no care for my own life. And for a while, I sought out the worst kind of pubs with the roughest of crowds in hopes I'd pick the right fight and someone would put me out of my misery. And instead, I nearly put someone out of theirs."

He could still hear the crunch of bone as the other man's body had slammed into a post.

As he spoke, Charlotte began moving again, methodically dabbing antibiotic ointment onto the cuts.

"If not for Peter Lennox, I'd probably be dead by now. He's the one who hauled me out of that hole. Gave me a new purpose. But I'm still that guy. I'm still that weak and careless man. Even now, I'm thinking about how good a drink would be to numb everything. I have that in me."

At last, she lifted her gaze to his, and the compassion he saw there all but undid him. She curled her hands around his. "You have trauma in your past. Trauma that you maybe didn't handle well, at the time. But you changed your life, made better choices. Today was horrible for all of us, so I'd be shocked if the temptation wasn't there. But you're not going to give in to it. Because that's not who you are. It's a thing you used to do. What you're going to do is pull everything together, because now that the police are involved, they know about Gavin. We both know that social services won't be far behind."

In all her ignorance of his past, she had such faith. But every single one of his failures was parading through his own mind, reminding him he'd never outrun that trauma.

"Maybe that's a good thing. Maybe he'd be better off with someone else."

Charlotte recoiled. "You don't mean that!"

"Aye, I do."

Her face twisted in shock, her breath wheezing out, as if he'd kicked her square in the chest. Because he was an asshole who hurt people. This little flirtation with the fantasy of a new family had simply made him forget that for a little while.

"Malcolm—" She reached toward him again, but he flinched back from the connection.

"Maybe you should go."

Temper and hurt warred in her expression before she slowly stood. "This isn't who you are, Malcolm. Not to me. Not to him."

They were wrong. They were both wrong. And as her quiet footsteps retreated, he reflected it was better for everyone that this should come out now, before major decisions had been made that couldn't be undone. Before he inevitably disappointed them both.

———

Charlotte hadn't slept. Every time she closed her eyes, she saw, not Simon threatening violence, but Malcolm giving up on everything. The family they'd built. Their fragile new beginning as something more. All the progress he'd made dragging himself out of the past, looking to the future, had been undone in one awful day. In so many ways, he was so strong. She hadn't expected him to be this brittle. He hadn't said they were over last night, but she knew. He'd retreated into himself, every single threat to his self-worth having convinced him he wasn't enough. Wasn't good for them. That she'd managed to overcome all that once was miracle enough. She didn't think she'd be able to manage it again. Wasn't sure her heart could survive the process if there was no guarantee he'd love her in the end, as she loved him.

But there was no time to wallow in her own heartbreak. Not with the worry about what would happen to Gavin. He'd been withdrawn when he came over this morning at the crack of dawn. Malcolm had taken himself off to the far ends of the estate, allegedly on business, but Charlotte knew he'd run away. From his feelings. From them. At least he'd made sure Gavin was safe, first. Worry made the boy look older than his thirteen years as they went through the routine of feeding animals, performing the chores that had become second nature. Completely understandable and expected after yesterday's events. But he still trusted that they'd keep him safe. That they'd keep the promises they'd made.

God, it would absolutely devastate him if he knew Malcolm had given up. She simply couldn't allow that to happen, so she had to pull an even bigger miracle out of thin air.

A sleek sedan pulled up in front of her flat, hopefully with a magician inside.

She was at the door, opening it before Hamish had even made it up the walk.

Charlotte had met the Edinburgh lawyer a few times since she'd come to Scotland. A Glenlaig native, he was Connor's best friend. The man who'd worked tirelessly for years to try to find a loophole in the marriage pact that had bound Connor and Afton. He understood complexities and the need to think outside the box, which was the only reason he hadn't sent them directly to social services in the first place.

"Thank you for coming."

"Of course." He stepped inside, his neatly pressed suit looking out of place in her casual living room.

"Gavin."

He rose from the kitchen table where he'd been mostly pushing around the breakfast she'd made for him. "Yes'm?"

"This is Hamish Colquhoun. He's the lawyer who's helping us with your case."

Hamish offered a kind smile. "Nice to meet you, lad."

Gavin edged closer to Charlotte and studied him with sober eyes. "Are you going to fix it so I can stay?"

"I'm going to do my very best."

Charlotte gave Gavin's shoulders a squeeze. "We've got a lot of boring legal stuff to discuss. Why don't you go check on the triplets? Give them a little romp in the yard out there?"

He squeezed her back, shooting another wary look at Hamish. "Okay."

Neither of them said anything as he pulled on his boots and headed out the door. Charlotte automatically moved to the window. She'd be able to keep an eye on him from here.

Hamish set his briefcase on the table, popping the clasps and removing a legal pad and pen from the interior. "Why don't you tell me what happened?"

"Okay. Do you want coffee? Tea?"

"I'd love some coffee, if it's no trouble. It was a long drive from Edinburgh this morning."

And he'd had to set out before the crack of dawn to make the trip this early.

With one eye on the window, she went through the routine of boiling water, setting up the French press. And she told him all of it, noting the faint scratch of his pen as he took notes.

When she'd finished, setting a steaming cup in front of him, he laid the pen aside. "Jesus. How is Malcolm doing after all this?"

"Not well at all. He's in a really bad headspace about all of it." Because grief about the whole thing threatened to drag her under, she curled her hands tighter around the back of the chair.

"I'm not surprised. I knew this would come up as we proceeded, but I didn't expect it to be like this."

"You know about all this?"

"Aye. It was part of the background check I ran on you both."

"What happened?"

Hamish hesitated. "He hasn't told you?"

"He told me some, but I suspect it was a biased account." She hoped it was, anyway.

"Well, the long and the short of it is that he was in a pub brawl. Multiple eyewitness accounts confirm that the other man started it. Kept poking at Malcolm, trying to get a rise out of him. Eventually, he said something that elicited a reaction. Malcolm turned, leading with his fists, and knocked the other man back—straight into a support column I doubt either of them knew was there. It fractured the other man's back."

"Jesus."

"He was held partly responsible and did some jail time for it. Peter Lennox was a friend. Ended up vouching for him and offering up the job here initially as a condition of his early release and parole. He's never set a toe out of line since. And for the past twenty years, he's donated a percentage of his salary to the care of the man he injured."

Charlotte scrubbed a hand over her face. It was awful. But it hadn't been malicious or deliberate. He hadn't started it. Yet he'd taken full responsibility, even going so far as to help monetarily provide for the man who'd antagonized him. That wasn't the behavior of a weak man.

Why couldn't Malcolm see that?

"He still blames himself."

"Aye, he would. For all his gruffness, he's not a man who enjoys causing pain."

She thought of the lambs. An apology meant to make her smile again. So much more than the minimally necessary "I'm sorry." That was the man she'd fallen for. The man she'd unhesitatingly stepped in to share a child with. But that wasn't who she'd seen last night.

"All this shit with Simon has brought everything back up for him, and honestly, I don't know if he's going to be able to pull himself out of it in time to deal with the custody situation. So we need to proceed with just me. I'm not letting anything happen to that boy. I know he's still here for the moment, but you and I both know it's only a matter of time before social services shows up to claim him."

Hamish's vivid blue eyes were kind. "I'll be honest. It's not going to be easy. You can't get certified as a foster parent in our country until you have citizenship, and that process alone could take months even before certification. Even if you were able to navigate all of those hurdles, there'd be no guarantee you could get Gavin back."

Back. Because the inevitable conclusion was that he'd be taken away no matter what.

She swallowed. "There has to be something. We can't let him go back there."

"I at least feel confident in giving you that assurance. Gavin's been gone from Duntyre for nearly three months. His father never reported him as missing and outright lied to the school when they inquired. Someone I trust in the system has already told me she's building a case against him. Now that they're aware of Gavin's location, there will be a court hearing to determine whether he should be formally removed from the home. Given the corroborating evidence I was able to provide and Gavin's own testimony as to his father's behavior, I don't think there's a chance in hell they'd put him back there. The difficult part is trying to keep him here."

Charlotte stared out the window where she could see Gavin wrestling with the triplets. Even amid all the chaos, they could wrangle a smile from him. "He's happy here, Hamish. He's safe and settled and healthy. Taking him away will only add another trauma, another loss, to a list that's already far too long." She turned her attention back to the lawyer. "What are our options?"

He laid out the problems, the challenges, the legal precedent. His list of solutions was painfully brief because the law simply wasn't on their side.

"I have a plan. It's not usual, but with the constantly over-worked and under-funded system, I might be able to convince the judge at the hearing that granting you the right to apply for a special guardianship order and allowing Gavin to stay where he is would save a lot of expense and trauma. Of course, that still depends upon Simon being willing to agree to it, which seems like a long shot, given what you've told me. Best-case scenario, he agrees, but we need Malcolm on board. We simply can't get a permanent residency status for you fast enough."

These were the impossible odds she faced.

Convince Malcolm to pull himself out of the pit in order to save Gavin, regardless of what it meant for their personal relationship, and risk that they'd get shot down anyway, which might do even more permanent damage to Malcolm. Or throw in the towel and admit defeat.

Charlotte didn't know how to admit defeat.

"Do what you have to do. I'll talk to Malcolm."

Thirteen

Malcolm's jaw throbbed like a bitch. So did his ribs. He knew from his brief glance in the bathroom mirror that he looked like absolute shite, despite Charlotte's ministrations the night before, and he embraced it. Why not have the outside reflect the pain he felt inside? He'd barely even been able to look at Gavin this morning, too afraid to see the disappointment—or worse, fear—in the lad's eyes. He'd sent the kid over to Charlotte's barely after dawn and taken the coward's way out, heading for work in the remotest parts of the estate. After everything that had happened, they wouldn't be left alone, and hopefully, Simon was still in jail for a few more hours.

He'd been over and over the whole thing a thousand times, searching for what would have been the better path. The one that didn't put the child or the woman he'd come to love in danger. But he hadn't found it by the time dawn began brightening the horizon. If he'd turned Gavin over to the authorities from the beginning, they might have sent him back to Simon or to one of the less-than-ideal care placements. Chances were, he'd have run away again, and might have run afoul of any number of dangers that could've left him injured, traumatized, or worse. Malcolm and Charlotte would likely still have been at some form of sniping impasse. And he'd have carried on in the self-isolation that had saved his sanity, his heart still encased in ice.

Much as he longed for that numbness, he wasn't willing to trade their safety to get it. So, no, he still couldn't see how he could've done anything other than exactly what he'd chosen. And the two of them had wormed their way into his life, bringing that frozen heart of his back to life. Over the past weeks, he'd begun to shed the armor he'd donned so very long ago. It had been terrifying and exhilarating. And for a little while, he'd believed it would all work out. That maybe he'd finally paid enough penance, done enough to earn some salvation, to deserve to feel joy again. He'd begun to cautiously build a future in his head, when he hadn't done more than look beyond the day or the season for decades.

But he'd been a fool, deluding himself that just because his position was morally right, the law would ultimately back him up. It had been a fantasy. One he'd embraced willful ignorance to maintain. And now, everything would fall apart. The threat of that inevitability had driven him to snag the whisky from the manor house. He hadn't wanted to go into the village with evidence of his current sins painting his face in vivid shades of bruising. Now that he'd done the essentials of his work, he'd settled on a rock overlooking the loch for which the estate was named. The bottle sat within arm's reach, as yet untouched as he wrestled with his demons.

He'd been wrestling with them for more than an hour. Long enough for his arse to go numb from where he sat on the cold stone, hunched into his jacket.

The rumble of an engine pulled him from his brood. He spotted another of the estate 4x4s coming up the narrow track. For a moment, Malcolm considered trying to hide the whisky. If it was Raleigh, that was hardly the best impression to give to his boss. But he was past caring. Maybe he deserved to be sacked so he could complete his descent into the pit of despair.

But it was Charlotte who slid from the driver's seat, mouth pressed into a grim line.

Instantly, he looked for Gavin, but she was clearly alone.

Alarm had him shoving to his feet as she approached. "Where's Gavin?" His pulse began to thud with dread. Had they already taken him? Had he lost his chance to say goodbye?

"With Raleigh and Kyla, for now. I need to talk to you."

Assured of a temporary reprieve, Malcolm turned away, unable to look at her because she represented too much temptation. Every cell in his body wanted to wrap her in his arms and take the comfort he knew she'd offer. To give the comfort she'd needed last night that he'd denied her. But he had to stay the course.

"I've already said what I have to say."

"Then you can listen, because I haven't." She came to stand beside him, looking down at the loch. "I met with Hamish this morning. He's confident that Gavin won't be going back to his father. There's sufficient evidence that the judge is likely to put him into foster care."

It was what he'd expected. The thing he'd been protecting himself from because the idea of losing another child absolutely cut him off at the knees.

"I'm pursuing special guardianship myself. Hamish is going to try to convince the judge to allow me to apply. I still have all the same things stacked against me. I'm not a UK citizen. I don't have permanent residency status. But I'm going to try." She turned to face him. He could see the pained lines of her face in his periphery. "And I'm probably going to fail unless you step up."

Tension hunched his shoulders as her words sank in. But she just kept right on talking.

"You and I went into this together from the very beginning. We were on the same page that we would do whatever is necessary to protect that child. He gave us the commonality of purpose to get over our antagonism with each other to find our way to something wonderful. And you're just throwing it away. Breaking that promise."

At her accusation, he spun. "You think I want to let him go? Do you think the idea of that disnae leave me gutted?"

"No. I can see that it does. Just as I can see that you've given up. That you are so mired in memories and regrets from your past, you can't see where you actually are. *Who* you actually are. So I'm here to tell you what I see. I see a man who unhesitatingly opened his home and his life to a child in need. Who overcame his natural reticence with people to be what that boy needed. I see a good father, a man who loves that child. A man I've grown to love. One who, I thought, cared for me."

Her voice hitched a little, and he had to curl his fingers into his palms to stop himself from reaching for her.

"I don't matter in this equation right now. The only thing that matters is Gavin. At the moment, I don't care what happens between the two of us. Whether we figure it out or we don't, I care about keeping our promise. We told Gavin that we would keep him safe. And the only way we can possibly do that is if you step up and do what you said you'd do."

"What is it you think I can do?"

"There's a court hearing tomorrow to have social services present their case against Simon. Hamish intends to present evidence that, despite all the legal precedent and the typical rules, the judge should allow him to stay with us. If it's just me, the effort will almost certainly fail. But if you're there, we stand a chance. Maybe it won't work. Maybe he's going into the system no matter what and we won't get to see him again. But at least he'll see us fighting to do what we promised."

Malcolm's chest tightened and his eyes burned.

Charlotte took a step closer and started to reach out. But she dropped her hand before touching him. "I know you're scared, and I know you're hurting because everyone who has ever mattered to you has been taken away or left. But I'm still here. And if you can get over yourself to do the hard thing, Gavin could be, too. The fact is, if you don't man the fuck up, you will wonder for the rest of your life if something could have been done differently, and I don't think you need any more ghosts."

When he said nothing, she glanced down at the whisky bottle a few feet away. "You aren't that man. Taking one night to drown in your grief doesn't make you that guy anymore. And the last twenty years count for more than the two you lost yourself."

His throat worked as he fought back emotion. He wanted to be the man she saw. Wanted to see himself as she did. But he didn't know how.

Compassion and temper warred in her face before she stepped forward and pressed something into his hand. "This is the time and location of the hearing. I hope we'll see you there."

Without another word, she strode back to the 4x4.

Long after she'd driven away, he was staring at the empty road, processing what she'd said. Charlotte had never been someone who shied away from the truth. It was one of the things he loved about her, even when he hated being forced to face it.

She was right. Of course, she was right. He was so afraid of losing more people, he was removing himself before they could leave him—willingly or otherwise. In his pain and fear, he'd pushed her away when she was arguably one of the best things to ever happen to him. He was risking breaking one of the most important promises he'd ever made to a child who'd only ever known betrayal and heartbreak.

Malcolm wanted to be better. He wanted to give Gavin someone to count on, to believe in. And he wanted to be a man who was worthy of the love of a woman with a heart as big as an ocean.

As the certainty of that settled over him, he knew what he had to do.

———

Why were municipal buildings always gray? Had there been some international decision to make them as lifeless and devoid of warmth as possible? To remove the humanity from the proceedings taking place inside?

Charlotte tightened her hold on Gavin's hand as they followed Hamish into the courtroom for the hearing. She hadn't wanted him to be here, but as she wasn't his mother, she didn't get a say. After her experiences with Raleigh, she ought to be used to that. Hamish had pointed out that the judge would need to speak to Gavin to get his side of things before making a ruling. She understood the necessity, but she hated the anxiety she felt radiating off him in waves. Hopefully it would be in their favor for the judge to see exactly how afraid he was of being in the same room as Simon.

A young woman with sandy brown hair and glasses sat at one of the tables in front of the bench. She rose at their approach.

"Hamish."

"Mhairi. I'd like you to meet my client, Charlotte Vasquez. And Gavin Elliot. This is Mhairi Mackenzie, from Children's Services."

Numbly, Charlotte shook the woman's hand. She was too nervous about what was coming. As Mhairi turned a warm smile on Gavin, he tucked in closer to Charlotte's side.

"It's nice to meet you, Gavin. I know all of this is scary, but we're all here to make sure you're best taken care of."

Not all of us.

Malcolm hadn't shown. Charlotte was struggling not to reveal her incredible disappointment. She'd really thought he was going to come through. That he'd pull himself out of the dark to do what was needed. The man she loved was capable of that.

But maybe it was just a sign that she didn't know him after all.

A door opened in the back of the courtroom, and she spun, her heart in her throat. But it wasn't Malcolm. It was Simon, swaggering his way to the front with all his bad temper on display. A harried-looking man with a bulging briefcase followed behind.

Given the wide berth he gave his client, Charlotte could only assume this was his public defender, or whatever Scotland's version of that was.

Simon shot a lascivious leer in her direction. It was made somehow worse by the broken nose and livid bruising of his face. She just tightened her arm around her quaking child and prayed.

"All rise."

As none of them were yet seated, they all turned toward the front of the court when the judge walked in. Her dark blonde hair was cut in a sharp bob that seemed to enhance her severe expression. With a glance out at the assembly, she nodded to herself and sat.

"You may be seated."

Hamish had already explained that, as Charlotte wasn't a legal guardian for Gavin, she wouldn't be able to sit beside him for the proceedings, but she could sit in the front row of the gallery behind the rail.

She gave him one last squeeze and pressed a kiss to his cheek. "It's going to be okay."

He looked like he wanted to bolt, but he sat instead between Mhairi and Hamish.

Charlotte took her place immediately behind him, her pulse jumping.

The judge opened her mouth to speak, but the door at the back of the courtroom opened. They all turned toward this latest interruption. Charlotte's heart shot into her throat as Malcolm strode down the center aisle. For the first time since she'd known him, he wasn't in a kilt. He'd worn a full suit, and he looked as uncomfortable as she'd ever seen him. His face was painted with violence, but his shoulders were square as he hurried forward.

At the judge's glare, he cleared his throat, tugging at the knot of his tie. "My apologies for being late."

He scooted onto the bench beside Charlotte and sat, leaning forward to squeeze Gavin's shoulder. The light and hope that flooded Gavin's face had tears filling her eyes. She couldn't say any of the things tumbling through her head, not with proceedings about to begin. But she took his hand, holding tight to those familiar, callused fingers. Malcolm's gaze met hers, full of apologies and things yet to be spoken. All things for later.

They sat that way, hands clasped, as Mhairi and Hamish presented the case for removing Gavin officially from Simon's residence. Though there was no direct evidence of abuse, the evidence for neglect was especially damning. The judge's face grew grimmer and grimmer.

"Have you anything to say for yourself, Mr. Elliot?"

Simon's attorney leaned over to whisper something.

Simon scowled. "No, Madam."

"Very well. This is a very clear-cut case. There is no question that the minor child should be removed from the home."

"Madam," Hamish interrupted. "I would beg the indulgence of the court to present some additional evidence."

"To what end?"

"Regarding gaining your permission for my clients to apply for special guardianship of the minor child."

"And your clients are?"

"Charlotte Vasquez and Malcolm Niall. The couple with whom Gavin has been living for the past five weeks."

The judge looked a little intrigued despite herself. "Are either of them relatives of the child?"

"No, Madam."

"Has there been any kind of child arrangements order granting them permission?"

"No, Madam."

"Are they foster carers?"

"No, Madam."

"Do they have the consent of either parent?"

"Hell, no," Simon burst out.

The judge's glare was swift. "Not another word from you, Mr. Elliot." On a sigh, she turned her attention back to Hamish. "Mr. Colquhoun, these are the bare minimum requirements for special guardianship. Why would you waste my time asking for consideration of this?"

"Because I believe circumstances warrant looking at the bigger picture. If you'll please give me a few minutes to present my case?"

The leather creaked as she sat back in her chair. "Proceed."

"My clients stumbled upon this child squatting in an abandoned crofter's cottage. Rather than react by turning him into the authorities, as if he'd done something wrong, they took him in. Fed and clothed him. Showed him the kindness he clearly wasn't receiving in the home he ran away from. For the past many weeks, they've given him shelter and protection and love, none of which they had to do. They have no obligation to this child. He is not of their blood. They gave him a home, anyway. They gave him a family."

"And disregarded all existing rules about how such a thing should be handled," she pointed out.

"True, but respectfully, Madam, they did it out of love and a desire to protect him. You and I both know that the system does the best that it can, but it's constantly overloaded and underfunded. Gavin is safe and happy with Mr. Niall and Miss Vasquez. Is it really necessary to traumatize him further by pulling him away from the only real stability he's known, from people who love and care for him, in the name of upholding the rules?"

The judge hummed a non-committal note. "Miss Vasquez is not a citizen of the UK. What's to stop her from simply going home to America?"

Charlotte couldn't stay quiet. "Family, Your Honor."

"I beg your pardon?"

"My son—my pseudo son—" Shit. How did she explain Raleigh with brevity?

Hamish smoothly interjected. "Miss Vasquez stepped in to raise her best friend's son after she died of cancer. That child is now the Baron of Lochmara. As such, she is pursuing citizenship."

When she didn't stop him, Hamish lifted a folder from the

table in front of him. "With your permission, I have a stack of affi-davits here. Character references as to the kind of parents Miss Vasquez and Mr. Niall make. Please review them. Talk to Gavin himself. I know that this is unorthodox, but I'm imploring you to save child services time and money, and save this child from the additional trauma of being ripped from the best home he's ever known."

The judge held out a hand, and he scooted around to take it to her.

No one spoke as she skimmed the contents. Charlotte was fairly vibrating out of her skin, trying to contain the hope rioting in her chest.

At last, the judge raised her head, her face softening for the first time all day as she looked at Gavin. "We've yet to hear from you, lad."

He shot a look of pure apprehension toward Simon. "I dinna want to talk in front of him."

Her face gentled further. "Okay. Then we'll retreat to my chambers for a private conversation."

She rose, and everyone else did, too.

Gavin turned panicked eyes to Charlotte. She and Malcolm each laid a hand on his shoulders.

"It's going to be okay. Just tell her the truth, baby."

"We'll be right here on the other side," Malcolm assured him.

With a nervous gait, he followed the judge out of the courtroom.

As soon as the door shut behind them, Charlotte turned to Malcolm. "You're here."

"Aye. I couldnae be anywhere else." His throat worked. "You were right. I was letting my fear and my past get the better of me. I'm sorry I lost faith. And I'm sorry I hurt you in the process."

She slid into his arms, holding him tight as the relief she hadn't quite let herself feel yet crashed through her. "You came. That's what matters."

He pulled back slightly, skimming a finger over her cheek.

"It's no' the only thing that matters. I'm here because I love you. I love him. And I want to make it work, whatever that looks like."

He loved her. She'd known it somewhere, deep down. Had felt it in his actions, seen it in his looks. But she'd needed the words. Needed, too, his assurances that he still wanted this family they'd made together. She knew what it had cost him to be here, to face his fears and step up. Love and pride geysered inside her, so much emotion for this perfectly imperfect man who was everything she hadn't known she'd been missing.

She tipped her cheek into his palm. "Damn it, don't make me cry right now."

Shifting, he pulled a handkerchief from his pocket. "I've got you covered."

On a watery laugh, she hugged him again.

They stayed like that for long minutes, waiting, until at last the door opened again and Gavin emerged, followed by the judge. He resumed his position between Hamish and Mhairi as the judge stepped back up to her bench. Charlotte and Malcolm leaned forward again, hands on Gavin's shoulders as they waited for the ruling.

"After consideration of the presented evidence and the testimony of the minor child, it is the opinion of this court that Mr. Niall and Miss Vasquez be granted permission to apply for special guardianship, and that he will be allowed to remain in their residence until such time as guardianship is confirmed."

All the stress and strain of the past days melted into relief. Gavin vaulted over the rail and into her arms. Malcolm wrapped them both in his. And surrounded by the family of her heart, Charlotte burst into tears.

EPILOGUE

Thanksgiving was Malcolm's new favorite holiday, even if they'd technically missed the actual day. The long table in the manor house dining room was groaning beneath the weight of all the food. Because cooking was what Charlotte did. To celebrate. To work off stress. To show love. As he benefitted immensely from this particular tendency, he wasn't about to complain. Added to which, he had so very much to be grateful for.

The center of it all was brandishing a wooden spoon when he stepped into the kitchen to see if they'd gotten all the dishes.

"Gavin Elmore, those rolls are for the table!"

Grinning, the lad ducked out of reach, tucking the breadbasket under his arm like a rugby ball. "Elmore?"

"Well, I don't actually know your middle name to properly middle name you, so I made one up on the spot," Charlotte admitted.

"It's Christopher."

Malcolm hooked him around the neck, drawing him in for a hug. "Maybe it's a good thing she didn't name you from birth."

Her cute little nose wrinkled in a snit. "I didn't say that's what I'd have *picked*."

Raleigh swung into the room. "Don't feel bad. She's always known my middle name, and she still liked to pull out weird ones when calling me out for stuff. I'll never forget Raleigh Louise."

She fixed him with a Mom glare. "You are not too old for me to whack with this spoon."

He just laughed and pulled her in for a smacking kiss on the cheek. "I love you, Charlotte."

She squeezed him back. "Okay, okay. All of you out. I just need to grab the gravy and we can eat."

Malcolm waited for all of them to exit before cornering her across from the stove.

"What? Did I forget something?" He could see the details of the meal scrolling through her brain again.

"No. I just needed to kiss the cook." Bending his head, he caught her mouth in a sweet, lingering kiss that had her melting against him.

"Mmm. Dessert first. No complaints here." She dropped back to her feet, eyes clearing. "Oh, damn it. I got potatoes on your shirt from my spoon!"

He chuckled. "Worth it."

She wouldn't let him leave the room until she'd dabbed at the stain.

Conversation was flying fast and furious around the table by the time they joined the others. Raleigh was at the head on one end. Charlotte took her position anchoring the other, and Malcolm sat beside her, across from Gavin. Everybody quieted as Raleigh tapped his water glass.

"Okay, Charlotte, this is your shindig. How do you want to do it?"

With an incline of her head, Charlotte accepted the role of hostess. "There are a lot more of us here tonight than you and I have had in a long time, and I already see you eyeing those sweet potatoes, so I'll keep this brief. Thanksgiving has always been an important holiday for Raleigh and me. In those first few years after his mama died, we had to work hard to find things to be thankful for because we missed her so much. But I knew it was something important to Lily, so I put in the effort as a way of honoring and remembering her. Over time, it's gotten easier. And though we are a very long way from Texas, and there have been so many changes, I felt especially called to celebrate this year. So, how we usually do this is to go around the table and take a few moments to say something we're thankful for and toast it. However much or little that may be."

She picked up her glass. "I'll start. First and foremost, I am grateful, as always, for my boy, Raleigh, for always treating me as family. For giving me this new home and the chance to build a new life. That new life has brought so many wonderful people into my world, including an entirely unexpected romance and a second son." Her eyes glittered as she smiled at him and Gavin, in turn. "I am especially thankful for Hamish, who went above and beyond to see that we can legally keep Gavin, and I'm thrilled to report that we'll be starting the formal process to make that permanent next week. Cheers!"

Answering cheers rang out around the table.

Gavin lifted his glass. "I'm thankful I got caught. I never dreamed I'd end up with amazing parents out of the deal." Ears turning pink, he shrugged. "Cheers."

Sophie went next. "I'm grateful for the exceptional success Kyla and I have had with our event planning business. It's been a whirlwind of a year, but I couldn't be more pleased. Cheers!"

Connor cleared his throat. "I'm thankful Afton made the hard choice to save us both, and that she managed to choose someone who was my sister's perfect match. You've been a hell of an addition to our lives, and I'm pleased to call you family. Cheers!"

"Aw hell, man, you're gonna make me all emotional." Raleigh wet his throat and continued. "Obviously, I'm thankful for the same. For the extraordinary woman I married and the incredible people and place we live in. The truth is, since I got here, I've faced all kinds of difficult decisions, having to dive in and learn things from the ground up in a way that was, frankly, intimidating. I've been able to get through that, in part, because of the support of my wife, but also because of you, Malcolm. Because you've been here from the beginning. Even when you didn't know quite what to make of me and my new ownership of Lochmara, you taught me so much. For a while now, I've been looking for an appropriate way to thank you, and I think I've finally hit on the right one."

Uncomfortable with the praise and attention, Malcolm shifted in his seat. "Thanks aren't necessary. It was my job."

"We can agree to disagree on that. If this doesn't work for you, we'll come up with something else. But I think this will be up your alley. First up, I want to give you a stake in the estate. You've dedicated the better part of your life to this place, and you deserve some ownership. Hamish has already done up the paperwork. Second—"

"Second?" Malcolm choked out. There was more?

"—with the permanent addition of Gavin to the family, the three of y'all are gonna need a bigger place. Somewhere y'all can all truly live under the same roof, while you're building your new lives together. There's a house out close to the loch. As most of them, it needs some work, and I'm happy to donate money, time, and effort to help get it up to Charlotte's standards. But with two stories and three bedrooms, I thought, if it suited all of you, it would make a fitting thank you from me to you, Malcolm, for all of your help and dedication to the estate, and to you, Charlotte, for being my second mom, and now Gavin's."

Malcolm's throat went tight with emotion. For all his gratitude to Peter Lennox, he'd never ever thought to have a stake in this place.

Beside him, Charlotte promptly burst into an ugly cry, all those big emotions spilling out. He reached over to clasp her hand, but kept his focus on Raleigh.

"I hardly ken what to say. This is... beyond generous. I know the house you speak of. It'll probably take a few months of work, while we're continuing on with all the other cottage rehab, but I know it'll be a good home in the end." He looked at Charlotte, tears streaming down her cheeks, into the curve of her smile. "One thing I've learned about Charlotte is that making a home is her superpower. Whether you think you need it or not."

A laugh interrupted the tears. "You needed it."

"Aye, I did. And I need you. So what do you say? Do you want to move in with me?" He glanced at Gavin and quirked a smile. "With us?"

She shoved out of her chair and moved to frame his face, beaming at him. "Yes, I absolutely do." Then she kissed him, to the cheers of everyone.

What a difference a couple of months had made. But as he wrapped his arms around the woman he loved, he knew it wasn't the time. It was the people. It was *his* people. His unconventional little family. He had no idea what he'd done to get this lucky, to earn this chance again. But he knew he sure as hell wasn't going to waste it.

———

Connor could hear the thump of music from the club from where he stood on the sidewalk in the frigid December air. It felt strange to be here, after so many months away. Once upon a time, he would've been down here in Edinburgh on the regular, seeking out female companionship. But life had been more than a little chaotic since he'd been freed from the marriage pact. Since Kyla married Raleigh. Since he himself found out about the debt hanging over the estate.

Now that the axe of the balloon payment on their biggest loan was no longer hanging over their necks, and now that he was no longer being coerced by duty to marry someone he didn't love, he figured it was time to get back on the horse, so to speak. New Year's Eve had seemed the ideal time. New Year. New Him. An opportunity to start over.

Hamish was meant to meet him here, to play wingman. Since his best mate had married more than ten years ago, they'd engaged in this particular bonding ritual less and less often. In truth, he was more excited by the idea of hanging out with his friend than finding someone to warm his bed for the night. Though Hamish had lived in Edinburgh for years now, Connor still missed him. He came home to Glenlaig as often as he could, but Connor knew that caused friction at home with his wife, who was city through and through. So he'd enjoy the night for whatever it brought.

But where the hell was Hamish? Connor hadn't seen his sedan in the car park. Maybe he'd taken public transit to avoid driving and was already waiting inside.

Pulling out his phone to text him, he realized he'd missed some texts.

Hamish: **Bad news. Freya is sick, and Dayna had some sort of hobnobbing business party she had to attend for work tonight. Can't find a sitter this late in the game. I won't be able to make it.**

He followed it up with a GIF of Joey from *Friends* sticking his head through a door saying, "Very, VERY sorry."

Well, damn.

He sent back a GIF of JD and Turk from *Scrubs* having a bromance cuddle.

Connor: **Of course, it's fine. I hope wee Freya feels better. Send her love from Uncle Connor.**

Hamish wrote back immediately. **Will do. She's got the narwhal plushie you gave her and is finally sleeping.**

Connor: **Not the New Year's Eve you were hoping for.**

Hamish: **No. But you make the most of it, aye? You deserve some fun.**

Connor took a selfie of himself saluting, then slid the phone back into his pocket and eyed the front door of the club where a steady stream of people had been walking in.

He'd done this for years, determined to experience as much

freedom and fun as possible before the cell door of an arranged marriage clanged shut and put an end to it. But he found that, without that desperation driving him, the idea of going on the prowl simply didn't have the appeal it used to.

Yet he'd come all this way. He might as well have one drink before he left.

The pulse of the music had him tapping his fingers against his leg as he wove his way through the crowd toward the bar. Everywhere around him, people were dancing and laughing, full of revelry. Normally, that would've energized him. Tonight, it made him twitchy. The press of bodies felt claustrophobic. He longed for the peace of his forge. Creating function and beauty with fire and brawn satisfied him in a way nothing else ever had. Maybe over these past months of secret, desperate work, he'd purged something.

Finally making it to the bar, he ordered a whisky, then leaned against the wood to wait.

Hands covered his eyes. "Guess who?"

The American accent with a Southern lilt had him flipping through his mental files, wondering who the hell this was. He lifted his hands, curling them around pale, slim fingers, and turned. The sight of her smiling face had a name flashing in his memory banks.

"Swayze Parish."

Her impish smile widened as she pulled him in for a hug. He returned the embrace, trying to remember exactly when he'd last seen her. She'd been on one of his tours a year, maybe year-and-a-half ago, and, at the end of it, they'd shared a delightful weekend on the west coast before both moving on. They'd corresponded a bit, and he'd followed her rise as a social media influencer, more out of curiosity and a desire to learn her methods than because he hadn't been able to let go.

"Connor MacKean," she drawled. "How the hell are you? Are you in town doing a tour?"

"No, not tonight. What about you?"

"Well, you know how much I loved Scotland the last time I was here, so I couldn't stay away. A friend of mine's getting married and looking to do a destination wedding, so I'm helping scout locations."

"Really? If the Highlands are on the list, my sister has an event planning business. We do weddings on our home estate. Complete with a six-hundred-year-old castle." Might as well put in a plug for the business. Swayze had the reach to really put Ardinmuir on the map for destination weddings.

"I will absolutely add it to the list. Do y'all have a website?"

He reeled it off as the bartender slid over his whisky. "So you've been doing well for yourself. All those sponsorships."

Pleasure lit her pretty features. "I'm surprised you knew. You haven't responded to my DMs in a long time."

A frisson of guilt tried to worm its way into his brain, but Connor refused to let it. He'd made the parameters of their weekend very clear, and then let their connection die what he thought was a natural death.

"My world's been pretty crazy. My sister got married, and my uncle had a heart attack."

"Oh no! Is he all right?"

"He is now. But it was a long recovery. That's part of why I'm in the city tonight. I'm free of nursemaid duties for a bit."

Swayze's smile turned flirty, and she trailed a finger along his arm. "You know, I had planned to look you up on this trip. You said if I ever came back through this way..."

He had said that.

It was crystal clear she'd happily go for a repeat of the time they'd spent together. She was fun, attractive. They'd been good in bed. She could be his entertainment for the night.

He opened his mouth to suggest it. "I'm really flattered, and I appreciate the offer, but I'm engaged."

Wait. What? Where the hell had that come from? It had been the fallback from before, on the rare occasions he ran into one of his former partners. And it had been the truth, of a sort. He had been supposed to marry Afton. But now?

Swayze blinked. "Engaged? I didn't think you were the settling down type."

Since he'd already started down the path with this lie, he might as well follow it through. "Aye, well, it's taken us years to work our way down to this point. We've been sort of dancing around each other since we were young."

"Well, I won't say I'm not disappointed, but I'm also not surprised. You're a great guy, Connor. I hope you and—" She was clearly waiting for a name.

"Sophie." It was the first thing to pop into his head.

"I hope you and Sophie will be very happy together." She lifted her own drink in a toast. "It was good to see you again, Connor."

Then she disappeared into the crowd.

Well, clearly, he wasn't in the mood to go on the prowl. He could just imagine how prim, proper Sophie Cameron would react to being cast in the role of his fiancée. She'd fall right down to the floor, laughing until she couldn't breathe. It wouldn't be the first time she'd laughed at his expense. With all the burdens she'd carried over the years, he'd been more than willing to put his own ego up as a target just to wrangle a smile out of her.

But she wouldn't find out about this one.

As Connor sipped his whisky, he automatically scanned the club. A couple dozen feet away, on the dance floor, he spotted another familiar face. His sister's ex, David Murray. Double the reason to get the hell out of here. He'd never had much fondness for the guy and was grateful Kyla had ended up with Raleigh. A woman moved into David's embrace, twining her arms around his neck as they swayed to the music. He pulled her in for a kiss.

Okay then. Apparently, he was getting out there again. Good for him.

As the kiss went on, Connor arched a brow. He saw more

passion on that dance floor than he'd ever seen this guy show Kyla. So maybe he'd finally found someone better suited.

Connor drained the last of his whisky, slapping the glass on the bar and turning to go as David and his date pulled apart, circling to the beat of the new, faster song. Light flashed, illuminating her face, and Connor froze.

Because it was Dayna.

Dayna Colquhoun.

His best friend's wife.

Choose Your Next Romance

Dun dun duh! I know. I *know!* You didn't see that coming (at least I hope you didn't). But obviously, if you've been with me from *Jilting The Kilt*, Hamish has to be single by the time his book rolls around and that takes time. So hold the tomatoes and don't get mad that they're Book 5. PATIENCE, DEAR READER!

Meanwhile, clearly Connor and Sophie are up next, and I can't *wait* for you to fall in love with *Playboy in a Kilt*.

And if you haven't gotten enough of Malcolm and Charlotte, check out their bonus epilogue here: https://books.bookfunnel. com/a-little-lagniappe/h3jqn3z30h

Meanwhile, if you're here for more grumpy soft for sunshine romance, check out *Second Chance Summer,* my RITA® Award Winner for Contemporary Romance-Short. Or perhaps you're into the banding together around a child for found family. You won't want to miss *Those Sweet Words,* of the Misfit Inn series.

Other Books By Kait Nolan

A complete and up-to-date list of all my books can be found at https://kaitnolan.com.

Kilted Hearts
Small Town Contemporary Scottish Romance

- *Jilting The Kilt* (prequel)
- *Cowboy in a Kilt* (Raleigh and Kyla)
- *Grump in a Kilt* (Malcolm and Charlotte)
- *Playboy in a Kilt* (Connor and Sophie)
- *Protector in a Kilt* (Ewan and Isobel)
- *Single Dad in a Kilt* (Hamish and Afton)
- *Kilty Pleasures* (Jason and Skye)

Bad Boy Bakers
Small Town Military Romance

- *Rescued By a Bad Boy* (Brax and Mia prequel)
- *Mixed Up With a Marine* (Brax and Mia)
- *Wrapped Up with a Ranger* (Holt and Cayla)

- *Stirred Up by a SEAL* (Jonah and Rachel)
- *Hung Up on the Hacker* (Cash and Hadley)
- *Caught Up with the Captain* (Grey and Rebecca)

RESCUE MY HEART SERIES
SMALL TOWN MILITARY ROMANCE

- *Someone Like You* (Ivy and Harrison)
- *What I Like About You* (Laurel and Sebastian)
- *Bad Case of Loving You* (Paisley and Ty prequel)
  Included in *Made For Loving You* (Paisley and Ty)

THE MISFIT INN SERIES
SMALL TOWN FAMILY ROMANCE

- *When You Got A Good Thing* (Kennedy and Xander)
- *Til There Was You* (Misty and Denver)
- *Those Sweet Words* (Pru and Flynn)
- *Stay A Little Longer* (Athena and Logan)
- *Bring It On Home* (Maggie and Porter)
- *Come Away with Me* (Moses and Zuri)

MEN OF THE MISFIT INN
SMALL TOWN SOUTHERN ROMANCE

- *Let It Be Me* (Emerson and Caleb)
- *Our Kind of Love* (Abbey and Kyle)
- *Don't You Wanna Stay* (Deanna and Wyatt)
- *Until We Meet Again* (Samantha and Griffin prequel)
- *Come A Little Closer* (Samantha and Griffin)
- *Just Wanted You To Know* (Livia and Declan)

WISHFUL ROMANCE SERIES
SMALL TOWN SOUTHERN ROMANCE

- *Once Upon A Coffee* (Avery and Dillon)
- *To Get Me To You* (Cam and Norah)
- *Know Me Well* (Liam and Riley)
- *Be Careful, It's My Heart* (Brody and Tyler)
- *Just For This Moment* (Myles and Piper)
- *Wish I Might* (Reed and Cecily)
- *Turn My World Around* (Tucker and Corinne)
- *Dance Me A Dream* (Jace and Tara)
- *See You Again* (Trey and Sandy)
- *The Christmas Fountain* (Chad and Mary Alice)
- *You Were Meant For Me* (Mitch and Tess)
- *A Lot Like Christmas* (Ryan and Hannah)
- *Dancing Away With My Heart* (Zach and Lexi)

WISHING FOR A HERO SERIES (A WISHFUL SPINOFF SERIES)
SMALL TOWN ROMANTIC SUSPENSE

- *Make You Feel My Love* (Judd and Autumn)
- *Watch Over Me* (Nash and Rowan)
- *Can't Take My Eyes Off You* (Ethan and Miranda)
- *Burn For You* (Sean and Delaney)

MEET CUTE ROMANCE
SMALL TOWN SHORT ROMANCE

- *Once Upon A Snow Day*
- *Once Upon A New Year's Eve*
- *Once Upon An Heirloom*
- *Once Upon A Coffee*
- *Once Upon A Campfire*
- *Once Upon A Rescue*

SUMMER CAMP
CONTEMPORARY ROMANCE

- *Once Upon A Campfire*
- *Second Chance Summer*

- *Once Upon A Campfire*
- *Second Chance Summer*

About Kait

Kait is a Mississippi native, who often swears like a sailor, calls everyone sugar, honey, or darlin', and can wield a bless your heart like a saber or a Snuggie, depending on requirements.

You can find more information on this *USA Today* best selling and RITA ® Award-winning author and her books on her website http://kaitnolan.com.

Do you need more small town sass and spark? Sign up for her newsletter to hear about new releases, book deals, and exclusive content!